Armageddon House

Armageddon House

Michael Griffin

UNDERTOW
PUBLICATIONS

First Edition

TRADE ISBN: 978-1-988964-20-1

LIMITED HARDBACK ISBN: 978-1-988964-21-8

Also by Michael Griffin

Far from Streets
The Lure of Devouring Light
An Ideal Retreat
Hieroglyphs of Blood and Bone
The Human Alchemy

ONE

SLEEP CHAMBER, LAKE VIEW

MARK WAKES AT 6:20 this morning, the same time as every morning, alone in a tiny room. The mural opposite the bed offers a view of a blue lake surrounded by trees. The image seems real enough to convince him briefly, at least while his mind is still partly blurred by sleep, that he's looking at a beautiful scene outside an actual window, not just a photograph on a wall. For a moment, the lake is a tangible place, very near.

As he rises into consciousness, Mark realizes it's impossible. So deep beneath the ground, there are no windows.

Every other room on this level is identical, other than the murals, all of which feature different nature scenes. That wall is always unobstructed by furniture, broken only by the door. The hallway outside makes a curve so long and gradual, it nearly completes a circle. Doors along both sides open to these rooms. A bed, a metal box to contain clothing, and a wall-sized image of a lake, a mountain, an ocean or a forest, serving in place of a view. Placement of the image opposite the bed ensures it's the first thing seen every morning. This may help alleviate the sense of confinement.

This whole place has a smell, or at least Mark believes it does. He's never mentioned this to the others. It's an odor of intrusive wetness, not unpleasant, but incongruous in such a deep, dry place. It's the kind of damp that might settle out of a pile of leaves in a grass field, or rain-soaked pine needles on a forest floor. Outside, that smell might suggest organic processes, a chain of life. Here, it makes no sense.

Mark isn't sure he remembers selecting this particular room. He can only guess his choice might have been driven by affinity for this particular flat, clear lake. Certain details persist when his eyes are closed, sometimes when he's not even in his room. The way the trees bounding the lake lean inward, conveying a sense of yearning, of striving to become unanchored and slide into the water. Though on some level Mark never completely forgets it's only a large photograph, often his subconscious operates as if he really might be living on the shore of some nameless lake, water teeming with life below the surface. A perfect plane of blue, bordered by living trees, encircled by walking paths of dirt and gravel, overlooked by other houses or cabins similar to his own, structures whose presence suggest the existence of others living nearby, strangers, potential friends, each living in their own distinct milieu of images, smells, memories. He's not alone.

Of course Mark doesn't live in a lake cabin. He lives down here. It's not that he's actually forgotten.

Another consideration in selecting this particular room may have been its placement near one end of the hallway's broken circle. The location offers proximity to one of the bath facilities at each end, as well as being the farthest point from where Polly and Greyson reside at the opposite extreme. That distance, the conscious decision to separate from the others by the greatest possible gap, demonstrates mutual respect and understanding of the individual's need for privacy. He and Jenna at this end, Polly and Greyson at theirs.

The others still seem to believe that Mark and Jenna share a single room, though Jenna sleeps across the hall now. He and Jenna go to some lengths to encourage perpetuation of this idea of themselves as an ongoing pair, but at the end of each day, after they return to this level, and to their end of the hall, they part and live separately. Without ever crossing paths, they share the bath and shower facility, designed to accommodate a much larger population, hypothetical residents of many rooms never occupied. Partitions, stalls and enclosures exist that would allow both to utilize the space simultaneously without coming into contact at all, without any chance of one embarrassing the other in the middle of some private or intimate act. To be safe, Mark and Jenna have worked out a schedule so as to absolutely avoid any possible conflict during use of showers, bathtubs, toilets, sinks and mirrors. It's best this way, a perfectly frictionless arrangement.

Because she requires more time to prepare, Jenna wakes twenty minutes earlier, showers first, then returns to her own room, where she finishes getting ready. On her way past, she knocks once on Mark's door so he knows it's his turn to use the washroom.

When he's ready, Mark waits in the hall outside Jenna's door, until together they climb to the next level, a common area called the Square Lounge. There they meet Greyson and Polly for breakfast and coffee every morning, and return some evenings to the tavern on that same level.

As Mark showers, the spray echoing within one of many indistinct tile partitions, steaming water spraying down from the shower head, he feels confused, even irritated, as to one specific matter of recollection.

When did he and Jenna stop being an actual couple, and start pretending?

Maybe they were never truly together. He worries their love affair, their physical and emotional intimacy, might be something he only ever imagined. A shared past once seemed solid, definite beyond question. He knows aspects of Jenna, intimacies he could never have discovered otherwise, but now worries he's only imagined this private catalog of images, tastes, smells, textures and sounds. Increasingly Mark wonders back to the beginning of his time here. He envisions days when he and Jenna were closer, his mind seeking back toward a time when existence made sense, when their interactions were natural, not made awkward by pretense. Without any need to worry about how they might appear to others, they enjoyed simply being together. His belief in this reality feels as true as anything he knows. Why, then, does he often fear these memories are nothing but a pleasant-seeming invention, a backstory his mind created to help explain the loneliness he suffers in his solitary room? Some actual cause must exist that would justify his pangs of longing for a woman who is always near, but separate.

To believe it was once an actual relationship that somehow ended makes more sense than any alternative explanation. While life may have shifted to become strange and bewildering, the solidity of matter and persistence of events and relationships used to be constant, solid, never questioned.

Mark wakes alone. He showers alone, returns to his solitary room, and dresses alone.

Then he steps out his door, takes four steps, and waits outside Jenna's room. His wristwatch, a bulky gold antique he himself repaired and restored somewhere else, a time long ago, says 6:53. Experience tells him she's nearly ready. In two minutes, maybe three, her door will open, she'll emerge, and together they'll make the short trip upstairs to Square Lounge. Side by side they'll come into view of Greyson and Polly, creating the impression of being a connected pair. Greyson and Polly will assume this couple spent the night together, just as Mark and Jenna assume Greyson and Polly did, despite not actually seeing them go into the same room, or climb into a single bed. The beds are so small, it's not impossible to imagine Greyson and Polly might prefer to sleep apart, but, crucially, there's no reason to assume so.

This cycle repeats. Mark wants to believe each day is exactly like previous days have always been, and it's only his mind that ever changes.

AN INTERLUDE

TWO CLIMBING STAIRS

Footfalls echo in the concrete stairwell. Mark leads while Jenna walks behind. Accumulating echoes create an impression of many footsteps overlapping, sounds of more than two people climbing. He knows she's still here. Less than a minute has passed since she emerged from her room to join him. This meeting and their departure together occurred so recently that although she's out of Mark's sight, and the sound of her behind him is disguised by an illusion of many conflicting steps echoing from different angles, he hasn't yet begun to doubt that she's actually still here.

Despite this tenuous hold on certainty, and only to preempt its breakdown, he pauses and bends as if to re-tie his shoelace. This brief delay allows Jenna to catch up. Her presence, though expected, does soothe and reassure him. His anxiety diminishes. Though Mark is closer to the inner rail than the outer, Jenna easily sneaks through the narrower gap to his left, and slips past him. Always petite, Jenna is lately thinner than ever before. For some time now—months? years?—she's been doing additional exercises, well beyond the required regimen. These changes in her body obviously please Jenna, judging by the form-fitting tops and tights she lately prefers. She often remains in workout clothes all day. If she becomes sweaty from exercise and needs another shower, she changes afterward into a new outfit, clean and dry but otherwise identical, as if another round of focused exertion is always likely.

Lately Greyson teases about "the new, skinny Jenna," remarks she clearly enjoys, despite pretending to be irritated. Mark hates Greyson doing this. He can't stand the idea of Greyson looking at Jenna, thinking about her, evaluating her body's shape. Worse,

Mark's own reaction to this makes him cringe with awareness that he himself is thinking of Jenna in exactly the same way. It's a form of possessiveness, no better than what Greyson's doing, but Mark can't stop.

A few stairs ahead, Jenna glances back. Straight blond hair falls across her eyes, and she pushes it back with one hand as she breaks into a run. "Come on," she says playfully.

Mark hates the idea of letting her get away. He doesn't want to enter Square Lounge alone, after she's already gone in. They're supposed to arrive together, or at least that's how routine and repetition have made it seem. He runs to catch up, feeling a desperate, almost painful urgency.

TWO

SQUARE LOUNGE, FIRES NEVER LIT

Square Lounge is an enormous five-by-five grid of sitting areas, surrounded by an outer wall comprised of large kitchen modules and a tavern. Each of the twenty-five discrete squares for gathering is delineated by a lounge in the shape of a broken circle, capable of seating twenty people. At the heart of each is a concrete island, serving as both table and enclosure for an open gas fireplace, whose fixtures are covered by translucent stones like milky, polished agates.

Only once has anyone ignited a fire in the fourth circle, the one at which they frequently sit, nearest their shared kitchen. At the time, Polly expressed anxiety about combustion within this locked, air-tight environment, and though Polly voicing worry has always been an occurrence so common as to usually be ignored, Greyson and Jenna must have agreed. The fire was extinguished. The subject has never again been discussed, though Mark might like to try the fire again. He imagines gathering around the flames for warmth, some chilly evening, leaning in close. If Polly and Greyson were elsewhere, had other things to do, he and Jenna might sit alone.

The problem has always been, there are never any cold evenings. The temperature here is always exactly the same.

As Mark and Jenna enter, Polly stands at the food counter along the far wall, making something in a blender. Mark is about to say good morning, when Greyson comes into view from behind a pillar, holding a glass of ice. Greyson is squat and stocky, heaviest of the four despite also being shortest. He's thick in the torso, all compact muscle, like an Olympic wrestler. His curly mess of dark hair, his swaying, bow-legged walk and perpetual crooked grin makes him look, in Mark's judgment, like an oversized toddler always on the verge of knocking something over.

Polly glances up, eyes pink and watery, as if she's been weeping. Her eyes often look this way, not only when she's just finished crying, or verging on doing so again. With a frown she lifts the blender lid, peeks in, then continues what she must have been saying to Greyson. "It's not isolation. Why do you keep saying isolation? There's four of us here." She fires the blender briefly.

On a cutting board on the countertop rest a paring knife and several apple cores. Polly is blending apples.

"What the hell?" Jenna gapes. "Where'd you get those?"

Mark has no idea how long it's been since he's seen fresh fruit or vegetables. Long ago, Polly abandoned her hydroponic greenhouse as a waste of effort, saying they could never manage to eat all the stores of frozen foods, enough to last the four of them a thousand years. Mark has always believed, and wanted to say, there's quite a difference between the frozen stuff and a crisp, fresh apple.

Greyson fills his glass with cola from a tap, as indifferent to what Polly's making as to Mark and Jenna's arrival. "I'm saying isolated because we're apart from humanity, like, no contact with anyone we knew before. Do you remember your family?" He sips. "I've pretty much forgotten mine."

"Isolation means something specific." Polly opens a drawer and pulls out a mesh strainer. "This ain't it."

"No," Greyson says definitively. "Even four people can definitely be isolated."

Polly strains the blended apple puree into a glass. She sniffs, unconvinced. "What are we even doing here, anyway? There aren't going to be any bombs, after all this time. This is so pointless, hiding."

"Bombs?" Greyson almost laughs, seeming to expect Polly to admit she's joking. He glances at Jenna and Mark, noticing them for the first time. "Poll, we're not hiding from bombs."

"Oh, really." She peers into her glass and sips. "What, then?"

Greyson answers with exaggerated slowness, as if speaking to someone dimwitted. "We. Are part. Of an experiment."

"Polly!" Mark shouts, trying to get her attention. "Where did you get the fucking apples?" He starts toward the refrigerators, thinking even if there aren't any more apples, he at least wants his usual coffee and protein drink.

Jenna registers mild surprise at Mark's forcefulness, but she too turns to Polly, clearly interested in this recently arrived fresh fruit.

Polly leans against the refrigerator and tries a playful kick toward Mark's thigh as he passes. "Just forget it, okay?" She takes another sip and seems satisfied, if not too excited. "If we start having to explain things to each other, there'll be no end to it."

Mark dodges Polly's kick, unsure what her remark is supposed to mean, and opens the second refrigerator in the row of eight. He and Jenna share the second, Greyson and Polly share the first, and the other six are unplugged, as are all the other refrigerators in the rest of the food prep counters lining the outer walls. Even though there's plenty of electricity to keep everything running, Mark long ago suggested shutting off redundant items in case spares are ever needed. In addition to thirty unused commercial refrigerators, they have a vast reserve of small appliances, kitchenware and utensils of excellent quality.

Avoiding Polly, Jenna circles the counter island in the opposite direction to join Mark at their refrigerator.

"Polly?" Mark insists. "It concerns all of us."

Polly glares down at her own feet and mutters, "Grow your own apples. Don't shake my tree."

"Just back off, dipshit," Greyson growls at Mark. "You drink that protein slop every day. What the fuck do you care about apples?"

Mark repeats himself, more slowly. "It concerns all of us."

Greyson shoves his way between Mark and Jenna, knocking Mark back into the refrigerator door.

"Jesus," Jenna says conspiratorially to Mark.

"Don't you love trying to coexist like this?" Mark whispers, intending only Jenna to hear.

"Everything's an argument," Jenna whispers.

"Or a contest," Mark adds.

Greyson laughs. "Contest, be glad it's not a fucking contest! The only contest you'll win is the wanking in your bunk contest."

Lately Greyson has been full of suspicious questions and accusations whenever Mark returns to his room during the day. In recent weeks, or maybe it's been longer, Greyson has begun raising the subject frequently, even when Mark hasn't mentioned the possibility of going anywhere. *Guess Mark's heading back to his room again, hoping nobody'd notice, eh, Mark?*

Mark glares, shaking his head. "What I work on in my room isn't for you to worry about, big guy."

"We all need our solitary pursuits," Polly says to Greyson, as if trying to calm him down. "Like my music, or your poems."

Polly transcribes music on paper, but because she possesses no instruments, nobody knows how the music sounds, except when Polly tries to hum or sing the melodies, at which times it seems she's unable to read her own notation.

Greyson scribbles thousands of short, experimental poems, entries in a numbered series he describes as "Meditations on Rage," which he leaves lying around the common areas, apparently hoping someone might read them.

Greyson tilts his head and gives Polly a nod, as if conceding the point. "Maybe, maybe so. Poetry does help me work through my antisocial impulses."

Mark makes an undignified snort.

"How lucky for us," Jenna observes brightly, "you working through those impulses. Otherwise, we might have to deal with your endless bullshit posturing."

"Posturing?" Greyson asks, seeming unsure whether to be hurt or angry. "What am I posturing like?"

"Phony, exaggerated masculinity," Jenna says. "Compensation for your shortcomings."

"Ooh!" Polly's eyes widen. She seems first delighted by the remark, then worried how Greyson might interpret her reaction. She looks down and away, now evasive.

Greyson glares at Jenna, then gives Mark the same hostile look. His face reddens and a vein in his forehead bulges. "Anybody who has any problem with my poems, anything I do, or anything I say, can fuck right off and stay the hell out of my face."

With a gasp, Polly drops her glass on the counter and begins flexing both hands in and out of fists, her usual mechanism for trying to calm runaway anxiety. "Greyson, we've talked, we've talked about this. We need to… we all need to…" She trails off and takes several rapid in-out breaths through pursed lips.

Knowing what's coming, Mark turns away. Polly is more apt to tilt from minor upset into full breakdown when she feels herself being watched. He fills a glass with ice and adds cold brewed coffee from a jar in the refrigerator.

Jenna too knows to look away. She dumps ice and two scoops of protein powder into a stainless-steel thermal cup, adds some of the cold coffee, screws on the lid and shakes it.

Even Greyson turns to focus on his food, drizzling syrup over ham and hash browns. He puts his plate into a microwave and pushes buttons.

In the background, Polly is hyperventilating. "It might be easier for me to cope," she gasps, "if you all let me in on the program."

Greyson groans. "The program again."

"Polly…" Jenna begins, obviously frustrated. "There's nothing we know that you don't."

"Yes." Polly nods vigorously, her face more that of a child than a woman in her thirties. "Yes, you do so."

"Your program," Greyson says, shrill and mocking. "You guys, your top-secret program!"

"Come on," Mark implores Greyson. "Don't make it worse."

Polly's cheeks go bright pink. She emits a cough-like sputter and bursts into full-on tears.

"Aww," Greyson baby-talks. "What's eating you, Polly-wolly?"

Polly shakes her head, emitting puffs of breath through pursed lips, trying to regain control.

Jenna approaches and wraps an arm around Polly. "Come on, girl."

Mark exhales, trying to dampen his own irritation. "Please." He wants to tell Polly they're all equally stressed. It doesn't help when somebody keeps breaking down emotionally every single day, constantly accusing the others of gaslighting her. "Greyson, you're making things worse."

Greyson takes his breakfast from the microwave. "It can't get fucking worse."

"God, I already need a drink." Jenna looks forlornly into her metal cup, then across the lounge toward the moody dimness of the corner they call Lonely Tavern, because there's no bartender on duty. It's the place they gather alternate evenings, each taking a turn serving the other three, who sit in the tall chairs, speaking to that night's bartender as if he or she were a stranger, a new arrival here.

Triggered by Jenna's suggestion and eager to soothe Polly, Mark almost suggests an impromptu bar session. Not only is it too early, but also the wrong day. Mark hates alcohol before a workout. Maybe they could skip exercise? He wishes Polly would get herself under control so they could return to their routine.

"You don't think we're against you," Greyson says to Polly, leaning in close, eye to eye. "You don't. You just pretend you do, because you want to draw attention to yourself."

Polly's hyperventilating and hand-wringing give way, and she spins, flinging both arms outward in anger, fluttering her hands, and bursts into another fit of sobs. "I'll do what I'm told, I'll be an asset to the project, I just … let me in on it, just let me in! Let me know secrets."

Her outbursts have been happening more often, and no longer only after they've all been drinking. Jenna has suggested to Mark, away from the others, that Polly only wants to gain attention, and doesn't really believe what she says, almost exactly as Greyson had suggested. Despite escalating tantrums, Polly otherwise remains friendly. Even after lashing out at Greyson, and despite his mockery at such times, they seem closer than ever, once her flare-ups subside.

Still, Mark questions how much he and Jenna really know about Polly and Greyson. He once suggested to Jenna that if the two of them were keeping secrets about their own relationship, maybe Polly and Greyson were, too. At that, Jenna lifted an eyebrow and stared as if she couldn't guess what he was talking about.

"The secrets," Polly whines, as if drawing out the words might unlock what they conceal.

"There aren't secrets," Jenna insists. "You know everything we do."

This may not be true, but Mark believes it best Polly continues to believe so.

Greyson is devouring his breakfast. "Nobody here knows shit," he says between bites large enough to choke a German Shepherd.

Mark drinks his coffee first, then blends a protein shake, while Jenna mixes the two together. They all eat and drink, standing in a row at the counter, Polly being pointedly ignored by the others, until the backdrop of her sobs and muttering gradually quiets, then stops.

Finally after a brief silence, Polly speaks. "Maybe I need new medicine." Blank-eyed, face slack with fatigue, she seems cried out. She bites into a dry onion bagel, and gazes down into her apple juice, but doesn't drink any more of it.

Sometimes out of nowhere, Mark finds a pull of attraction to Polly. Red-haired and freckled, with a build more strong than graceful, she differs from his usual preferred type. Physically, Polly's a better match to Greyson, and usually, Mark remains focused on Jenna. Still, he guesses it must be normal for a man locked away with two women, if he's no longer intimate with the one, to start wondering about the other.

"Speaking of meds, time for the daily doses," Greyson says, now done with breakfast. "Ready or not."

"I didn't mean our usual medicine." Polly sets the juice glass on the counter forcefully, making such a loud crack they all flinch, though the glass doesn't break. "I need something stronger. For my moods."

"Maybe you need a solitary pursuit," Mark says, and immediately regrets it.

Jenna elbows him in the ribs. "We'll sift through those old supply rooms on four, Polly." Jenna alone refers to levels by number, the highest being one, the lowest nine. "We haven't searched there in a while. Maybe we'll find medicine different from what's in the med lab."

"We can?" Polly asks in a baby voice. "You guys promise?"

Greyson sighs. "We can look, but we're not going to find anything."

"We'll all help," Mark agrees.

"Okay." Polly nods. "Everybody helps, you promised. Good. That's good."

MICHAEL GRIFFIN

AN INTERLUDE

FOUR DESCENDING STAIRS

Mark becomes lost in a swirl of footsteps echoing in a concrete stairwell. How can so many people make walking sounds all at once, in such a narrow space? Only four people exist, but they sound like many.

"We will," Greyson says. His words repeat and circle back. "We will, we will, but later, later."

At first Mark's unsure what's being discussed, until he returns to now, and here. He remembers some of what the other have been saying while his mind has been elsewhere. Polly keeps insisting over and over that the others renew their promises to help her look for new medicine. Every time, the others offer reassurance that they fully intend to help as soon as other obligations are finished, and Polly is only briefly appeased before she asks again.

"It's just, what I'm taking isn't enough," Polly says. "Obviously, I mean, just listen to me. All crazy over here. Totally crazy, this girl. It's so stupid. It's really dumb."

"We have to take our regular meds first," Mark says. "That, we can't skip."

"Not only that," Jenna adds. "We have to exercise after. And you're not dumb or stupid, Polly."

On the next landing, the residential level, they pass the steel door which has been propped open forever. They continue past and down.

"No, exercise later," Polly insists. "You guys promised. Exercise later."

Mark wants to repeat his insistence on handling obligations first. Med center, then Gymnasium, then only after that's resolved,

29

they can help Polly dig through disorganized boxes in long-forgotten storerooms. The burden of routine weighs upon him, yet he feels no escape is possible.

"Fine," Greyson concedes, deciding for all. "We'll take our regulation meds, then go find whatever else you need."

"Okay," Jenna agrees. "We can work out later."

At first, such an unexpected change in plans feels like a disruption, but now that others have given permission to break from routine, Mark experiences the lightness of relief.

THREE

MEDICINE CENTER, VIBRATING MACHINES

The tile walls and floor of the Medicine Center are brilliant, reflective white. Hot glare burns down from powerful halogen lamps recessed in the ceiling. Just like the tavern lacks a bartender, no doctor is present to dispense required daily medications. Each of the four has always known, without remembering ever having been told, which bottles they need, and in what dosages. They self-administer shots, or count pills to be swallowed with water. Each sits in their own elegant white leather reclining chair, Bauhaus-inspired works of functional art, all in a row.

Beside each, a stainless-steel tray organizes the day's medicines. Their remaining supply, sufficient to last years, is kept within glass-fronted coolers along one wall. Further back, a massive freezer stores deep overstock for the longer term, though Mark imagines none of them want or expect to remain here long enough to deplete the refrigerated supply. He takes this as given, that they will never need to delve into the deep-freeze, though nobody ever talks about how soon they might be able to depart.

Beyond the coolers, nearer the freezer, stand a dozen coffin-sized stainless-steel cylinders, which resemble vertical tanks of pressurized liquid gas, but bear no markings to indicate what they might contain. An intense hum emits from these, causing uncomfortable vibrations in the gut of anyone who approaches within arm's reach. Mark once briefly rested a palm on the first cylinder, which churned as if it contained some terrible, wobbling engine about to break loose and crack the metal shell like a hatchling emerging from an egg. A violent buzz threatened to shatter his bones and disintegrate soft tissues. Teeth chattered wildly and vision blurred until finally, on the verge of irrevocably losing all sense of himself, he stepped back.

Now everyone steers clear of that part of the room. Nobody mentions the cylinders, which never stop humming.

Each of the four focuses on their own medicines, pretending to ignore what the others are giving themselves, and in what dosages. Mark can't recall being told not to share these details, yet another matter they never discuss. The others seem to agree, discretion helps avoid trouble.

"Wait a minute, just wait. Say what?" Greyson directs these remarks toward Jenna, in response to some comment Mark must have failed to hear or register. "Exactly what do you think is happening here? God, you're as bad as Polly with this loony shit."

Jenna glances half-lidded at Mark, then back at Greyson. "All I said was tests, Greyson. God, you're such a hopped-up asshole when you're dosing."

Mark assumes all he missed was Jenna's vague theorizing about all of them being test subjects. It's a notion all of them have asserted at various times, even recently.

"No, no. Just no." Greyson sits upright, turns and straightens so his pink, hairy feet are on the floor. He's breathing fast, and seems tense and angry. A drop of sweat arcs down his forehead to his temple. "We're not at home, we're not going to work at jobs, living lives, coming home to families. What we're doing here is… No, I want you to say it, Jenn-Jenn. Tell me what you think this is."

Jenna inhales slowly, and as she exhales, relaxes her shoulders. "We're in a test facility, we're far underground. Can we agree on that much, or do you need to fight over every detail?"

"No, no." Greyson shakes his head in sputtering, unreasonable anger. "Just fucking no."

Jenna remains focused on her breathing, practicing an approach to calm mindfulness she once tried to explain to Mark. "Yes. And can we further agree that we all know perfectly well that we're far removed from the world?" She phrases this as a polite question, but in a tone that suggests nobody should bother disagreeing.

"Very far," Polly agrees, eyes still closed.

"Wait, just one fucking second. What does that mean, far from the world?" Greyson's voice is unusually high, as if he feels more threatened than angry, and wants to distract himself from that fear. He's rigid from neck to shoulders, grinding his jaw like a speed freak. "So you're saying, not only far below the surface, that's not far enough removed from humanity, right? They've also got to bury us, where? In such a remote fucking nowhere spot on the map that even if we did ever climb out, we'd die before we could walk to help?"

Polly opens her eyes and looks around. "Climb out, Greyson?"

"Nobody's climbing out." Mark restrains an urge to elaborate. "Nobody's walking anywhere, until it's over. Have you seen that outer door?"

Jenna continues smiling in a way that seems designed to show Greyson he's not getting to her. "Mark's right. We're locked in."

"You know, actually, I think we aren't the real test, ourselves," Polly interjects. "We're like a simulation of the big test they'll do later, somewhere farther away. Isn't that right? Like, a test for a test. I mean, humanity is just a trial run anyway. Preliminary, that's the word. Preliminary test. Each test is practice for another test, and that's practice for the next one. Only, how many? Like, which one is this?"

Still reclining, Jenna extends her right arm toward Polly in a gesture of solidarity or connection, even though they're too far apart to touch. Her eyes remain dreamy, as if she's submerged in warm bliss, not in the middle of yet another tiresome argument. Maybe her medications boost her ability to detach from conflict.

"Somewhere farther away, like where?" Greyson insists. He settles back, trying to recline again. "Siberia? Venus? Jesus, you fucking people. All three of you think this is something completely different, but somehow you're all in agreement that I'm the only one here who's wrong about things."

"Questions to be answered include," Polly says, as if reciting from memory, "what are the effects of spacial confinement, of social constraint, of aesthetic limitation, of restricted air and sunlight, of adherence to shifted chronological cycles, after one month's duration?"

"A month, is it?" Greyson snaps, whipping back and forth to glare at each of the others in turn. "Who said a month, who said any specific amount of time? When did anyone ever say that?"

"Don't be so defensive about forgetting," Polly says. "We all forget things, more and more every day."

"It's a designed, utopian environment, like a pleasure vacation," Jenna says with a little shrug, seemingly still untouched by Greyson's game of escalating anger and belittlement. "With a bit of work and routine obligation mixed in, to make life feel normal, so we remain balanced."

"Utopian, what the fuck?" Greyson says in disgust. "This resembles utopia in absolutely no way at all. I can't believe you even use that word here, buried down in this fucking shit-basement. Pleasure vacation. Psssh." In disgust, he reclines so abruptly and with such force, he strikes the back of his head on the chair's metal frame.

Mark feels an urge to stand, to rise from his chair and take some physical action against Greyson's bullying. Usually Jenna speaks up quickly to smack Greyson down, but she's peaceful now, eyes closed, apparently focused on Zen-like detachment. Mark finds it easier to let these aggressions pass when Jenna immediately puts Greyson in his place. But this quiet aloofness of Jenna's, while it might work for her, leaves Mark wishing someone would knock Greyson down a notch or two. He should be the one to do it. Jenna has never needed defending. No, he should calm down. He wants so badly to lash out, to do something, anything. At least words.

"You guys, things are getting worse," Polly says. "We're basically hostile all the time."

"Hostility destroys any possibility of settling into stable life," Jenna says, eyes still closed. "When every minute there's a new fight, adrenaline pumps nonstop. The atmosphere we breathe becomes poison."

"Not everyone here is confrontational," Mark says. "Only one of us."

"Whatever makes you feel superior, kiddos." Greyson exhales noisily, and crosses forearms over his eyes as if the light bothers him. "The human animal is nasty, especially in captivity. Sorry if I'm not willing to submit myself to the fake, phony bullshit like you all."

"Jenna was right before, Greyson," Polly sing-songs. "You're just compensating for shortcomings. Pathetic shortfalls in key areas."

Mark laughs, but wishes he could let it go. It may be satisfying, seeing childish shots landed on Greyson, but they all know it'll only lead to escalation and payback. He swallows his last pill, closes his eyes, and tries to remember what Jenna always tells him about relaxing through meditation. Anything to calm his nerves, stop the trembling. Only a few minutes rest remain before it's time to get out the blades.

AN INTERLUDE

LOST BLOOD AND DISCARDED FLESH

Today is Mark's turn in the rotation for biological disposal.

The others leave without cleaning up after themselves. After they're gone, Mark uses tweezers to gather organic detritus from each work stand into the larger stainless-steel tray atop the roll cart. Tiny snips of detached skin, unwanted eyelids, lobes and appendages, discarded trimmed nails, hairs and eyelashes pulled out by roots, all the flesh scattered amidst blood smears and spatters. Every day, the shedding of these parts leaves behind more waste than all the days before. This avalanche of decay, a kind of incremental death, is necessary for the renewal it brings. Each morning's birth, nearer and nearer to something new, and possibly final.

Usually the mess doesn't bother him, when it's his turn. Today he averts his eyes as much as possible. Imagining a smell, he holds his breath.

After he's gathered the many, variant traces of human matter, he wipes down chairs and work surfaces with disinfectant solution, which evaporates into eye-burning fumes. He mops the surrounding floor tiles with ammonia. After the vapors subside, a sense of clarity begins to emerge. Vision sharpens.

The wall-mounted incinerator opens like a windowless oven. Inside is yesterday's tray, now cool, bearing only a trace of sterile ash, easily rinsed away. He removes the clean pan and replaces it with today's, which bears the last, unwanted remnants of who they were until this morning, and never will be again. He closes the incinerator door. The latch clicks.

The black button must be held for five seconds to start the flames. Mark continues counting, six, seven, even after he hears the whoosh and feels the fire within roar to life. The metal door, now vibrating, begins to warm.

Despite the airtight seal, Mark is certain he smells life burning away.

FOUR

SUPPLY ROOM, GAS MASKS AND SALT RATIONS

By the time he's finished, the others have already begun exploring the supply level. Items stored in the various rooms would seem to be organized by age, rather than category or function, as if new rooms were added one at a time, and old stores ignored and abandoned as replacement items arrived at each time of expansion.

Mark hears voices from a room a few doors down from the stairs. Just inside lie dozens of green foil bricks of vacuum-packed coffee spilling from a decades-old cardboard case. Other torn and broken boxes dump varied contents across the floor. All the rooms are the same, this combination of unwanted mess with a sort of organization superimposed upon it.

"Boys and girls," Mark says, announcing his arrival.

Jenna turns and offers Mark one of two boxes she's holding. "Thirty-two ounces iodized salt," she says.

"Why do you suppose it's arranged like this, with so many small storage rooms?" Mark asks. "It's almost like residents gets their own room for sleeping, and their own storage closet up here." He holds onto the salt until Jenna drops her box, and only then discards his own.

"Maybe they were smart enough to realize nobody'd trust anybody else," Greyson says. "Best to keep everything separate."

"They?" Polly kicks through fallen boxes along the far wall. "Who's they?"

"Whoever built this place," Greyson answers. "At least, whoever planned it. But why should we need to guess? What's the point of making us figure out every detail on our own? We should've been told." He gestures widely, seeming to indicate all levels, above and below.

"Some of us were told," Jenna says. "One of us."

Mark assumes she's referring to him, and makes a point of nonchalant non-reaction, pretending he hasn't heard, or that this suggestion of his greater knowledge is something he too takes for granted. Though he's always considered himself insightful as to reasons, explanations and rules, nonetheless he's also often confused, especially lately. At times when he feels the least certainty, and the most disorientation, he tries to overrule the tug of rootless fear by asserting greater confidence. When feeling lost or afraid, he tells himself he knows every room on every level well enough to draw a map from memory. When he's terrified of the unknown future, he reassures himself that all anybody ever needs to do, all any of them ever can do, is see and hear what's right before them. Nothing important exists beyond what their senses describe of their immediate surroundings.

This isn't because he wants to lie to the others, or pretend he's something he's not. All he wants is to avoid letting dangerous ideas take hold and run wild. Uncertainty is like that. Fear is corrosive.

They search, kicking through disgorged contents of broken containers. Odd survival goods, obsolete rations fallen from broken-down shelves. Dozens of black rubber gas masks tossed in a heap. A jumble of giant syringes in sheaths that resemble transparent cigars. Thousands of boxes of bullets in obscure, non-standard calibers, mounded into pyramids. The mess seems orderly, not random, as if the larger boxes and the smaller packages they contain have been gone through, evaluated, pillaged for anything of value, then sorted before being discarded into heaps against walls or in the center of the floor. Any organizing principle that might exist seems difficult to guess. Mark doesn't believe anyone now present was involved in this sorting, but who else could it have been? The only explanation is that someone else was here before. Every item in this room appears far older than any of the four now present. Mark thinks he's oldest, at thirty-nine, but then he wonders if he's actually thirty-nine, or possibly older. Shouldn't a person remember turning forty? For a long time he's been thinking of that milestone as something just ahead, but now he wonders if maybe it's behind him.

"It's so damned fucking weird, this place," Greyson says. "I don't need every question answered, like Polly-wog here, but one thing I do know is that we're all four of us victims of some bad, unfair shit."

"Don't call me that," Polly says. "You suck sometimes, you know."

"That reminds me, Greyson, you were going to let us in on your big theory." Mark hopes to prod him into saying something outlandish enough that the others can make Greyson feel foolish and ridiculous.

"Since the rest of us are so wrong," Jenna says.

"So then, we're victims of bad, unfair shit, you say?" Mark continues. "Such as what, exactly?"

Greyson sniffs, kicking through the mess on the floor, but only pretending to look. "Tests, mostly psychological. But physical too, all that exercising. What possible need is there, hooking us to treadmills like fucking rats?"

Polly kneels before a pile of adhesive gauze bandages so old they've turned dark brown. She coughs, waving away dust. "I thought the drugs were meant to help them deal with isolation. I mean, help us deal with it."

"I don't believe the meds are even supposed to help," Jenna says. "Mostly they make me want to kill myself."

Polly grins and winks theatrically at Jenna. "Imagine how fucked up we'd be without 'em, though."

"I never wanted to kill myself." Greyson says, his grin demented. "I want to kill all of you."

"We each decided to be part of this," Mark says, "but you're the only one taking it out on others." He speaks without facing Greyson directly.

"I never decided anything," Greyson says. "We're torture subjects, worse than prisoners. You're just brainwashed."

Polly drops a faded carton of Chesterfield cigarettes and whirls to face the others, as if remembering something. "Hey, what ever happened to remote viewing, wasn't that a thing we were doing? Or did I dream it?"

Mark looks to Jenna, wondering if maybe Polly's joking to lighten the mood.

Jenna lifts an eyebrow. "Okay, my remote view is, this is boring. Can we go now?"

"You guys, no!" Polly whines. "You said you'd help me get some special medicine. There's a million more rooms to search. So many."

Greyson offers her an enormous box of hardtack crackers and a glass jar containing 1,000 tiny aspirin. "Try these," he deadpans. "And don't forget your solitary pursuits. But not the kind of solitary pursuits like Marky-boy pursues."

"Here!" Polly exclaims, as she bends to retrieve a brown glass eye-dropper bottle. "Yeah, this! This is it."

Mark squints at the dusty bottle, which bears no label and looks like it came from an old-time apothecary's medicine bag. "Polly, you sure? What even is this stuff?"

Polly nods, giddy with excitement. "This is the perfect thing, exactly what I need. I'll take some drops, then let's everybody go lie in the sun, okay?"

The others assent without argument. Mark agrees it's safest to return as soon as possible to the disrupted routine of breakfast followed by Medicine Center followed by Sun Room followed by Gymnasium. Not for the first time, he finds himself thankful that whoever set their schedule knew better what they really needed than any of them could possibly know for themselves.

MICHAEL GRIFFIN

AN INTERLUDE
SECRET BULLETS

Just before they reach the stairs, Mark stops. "Forgot something I wanted. I'm going to run back, only take a second."

He jogs back toward the supply room, not knowing whether the others will continue without him. Assuming they'll wait, he needs to conceal what he's returned to claim. He tears open a packet of hardtack crackers and dumps a few onto the floor. Nearby, he finds a particular box of bullets, the measurement 7.5mm the only comprehensible text among other inscrutable printing on the box. He drops four bullets into the open space in the packet and folds shut the end.

The others are still waiting, and turn to look as he jogs back.

"You didn't have to wait for me," Mark says, holding up the faded package of stale crackers.

Greyson makes a face. "Nasty." He heads into the stairs.

"Those can't be safe to eat," Polly says.

"Everything here is safe," Mark says. "My crackers and your Laudanum, both as fresh now as on creation day."

"I should've taken those accounting books," Greyson says.

"Absolutely," Jenna says. "Never too late to pass your CPA exam, big guy."

When they reach the residential level, Mark stops. "You go ahead. I'll stow this in my room and see you at the pool."

Though the others proceed without him this time, once in his room, Mark remains cautious, making sure the door is shut and latched before he kneels to open his trunk. In the bottom rear corner, beneath folded clothes in tidy piles, he conceals the bullets next to the old 7.5mm revolver already hidden.

FIVE

SUN ROOM, SWIMMING POOL

By the time Mark arrives, Greyson has already changed into his tiny, lemon-yellow racing swimsuit. It's far too small for any grown man, certainly for Greyson's broad torso and stout, hairy thighs. Mark looks away as Greyson jogs to his favorite chaise at the far end of the poolside row, as if someone else might steal his spot if he doesn't hurry.

Jenna and Polly remain before their open lockers, both still halfway through changing. Jenna wears only a black bikini top, having pulled down her gray workout tights and panties but not yet stepped into her bikini bottom. Leaning close to the mirror mounted inside the locker door, she scrutinizes her left eye, as if some detail there bothers her. The stark contrast of her tan lines is accentuated by her thinness. A hipbone crest shows like a blade beneath her flesh. It feels wrong, scrutinizing her so closely, though she makes no effort to hide herself.

Polly stands topless, adjusting bright orange boy-shorts so they're hiked up high enough, but not too high. Her freckles stand out in striking contrast against her pale breasts, though obsessive daily tanning has helped the freckles blend into the darker skin of most of her body.

Mark thinks it's strange, the way their rules of interaction shift here. There's no other place they casually expose themselves, not the Medicine Center, nor the Gymnasium. How is it they've fallen into distinct routines, which vary according to setting? Beside the pool, under glaring light, they disrobe without hesitation. Here, being revealed is nothing to worry about, while in every other place, they guard their privacy.

Is he the only one who thinks about this, or even notices? Mark feels awkward suddenly, as if the others might perceive him focusing on their nakedness. He commands himself to stop dwelling on it, and strips off shirt, pants and underwear. His green swim trunks aren't too large, but they seem oversized, being so much more concealing than what the others wear.

The Sun Room pool is a uniform five feet in depth. Along the near side, four dozen white lounge chairs stand in three rows of sixteen. Opposite, a back-lit glass wall slopes upward, curving at the top to merge with the ceiling. Behind the glass, an array of tiny, brilliant sun lamps automatically switch on whenever motion is detected. Thousands of pinpoints, made of some light-emitting material which radiates heat, as well as broad-spectrum light. When Mark closes his eyes, he can't distinguish the experience of lounging beside an underground pool from that of sunning on the surface, beneath a real sky. He tries to remember what it's like, looking up at the sun, a discrete circle overhead. These lamps never burn out, apparently never need replacing, and emit a wavelength that minimizes sunburn while offering the same vitamin D benefits as sunlight. Mark doesn't recall where he learned this, whether he arrived with the information, or someone mentioned it.

They all visit the Sun Room daily, not always all four together, as with so many other activities and settings, but sometimes in pairs or even alone. Just as Jenna often does an extra round of exercise on her own, Polly often revisits at odd hours. Today, they lie grouped together, wire mesh lounges almost touching.

After a few minutes, dizzy from the heat, someone moans.

"Mmmm, it's so hot."

For long seconds, nobody moves or speaks. Mark's eyes remain closed, but he can hear.

Polly shifts slightly. "Sometimes I wish we could turn it down a few notches, maybe half as much sun. It's nice, feeling warm, but I can only take ten minutes before I want to swoon."

Nobody responds, but Mark continues thinking about heat.

"Black became the sun's light…" a voice says.

Mark sits up, blinking, trying to see clearly enough to discern who was speaking. "Who said that?"

"Said what?" Polly asks.

Mark looks at the other three, trying to read them. "Something about, black becoming... the sunlight?"

Jenna sits up, removes her sunglasses. "Black became the sun's light, until in summer, all the world is storms."

"Was it you who said it before?" Mark asks.

"No." Jenna turns face down and unties her bikini top so the straps won't make tan lines on her back. "It's an old poem, from when the world ended. Don't you ever read?"

Sweat trickles down Mark's sides. He lifts himself, skin sticking to the mesh of the lounge, and gently turns over. "Does anyone hear that?" he asks without looking up.

Another gap of time passes.

"Hear what?" Jenna asks.

Mark realizes he asked about hearing a sound without having first decided it was a good idea to admit he was hearing something. But he's certain he still hears it, so there's nothing wrong with having mentioned it. "That trickling," he says. "A trickling sound."

"We're beside a pool," Greyson says. "It's full of water."

"The pool is motionless," Mark says. "Nobody's been in the water for days. The pool isn't the sound. I still hear it, just... Somewhere else."

"Somewhere else," Polly intones with solemnity.

"From above, like a leaking pipe, or maybe a crack in the wall. Or from below." He closes his eyes again.

"There are no cracks," someone says.

He thinks he knows everyone's voice, but sometimes when people say things when he's not looking, he can't picture which of them is talking.

A breeze sweeps past, a chill causing Mark's arms to tense. Skin on his flank constricts like gooseflesh. The sharp wind fades, surges, then disappears. Despite the heat of the lamps, Mark feels uncomfortable, skin exposed this way. And that smell again, the smell from his room of unexpected dampness. It seems like outdoors, like a place and time he remembers. He wants to ask the others. Why hasn't he asked before now? But he just mentioned the trickling sound, and nobody else heard it. That's why he doesn't say what he smells, what he remembers, what he sees or hears or anything else. There's no reason to reveal himself. Sometimes it's as if he's here alone, like all four of them are dwelling in their own separate worlds.

"This is the first time I've felt right in a while, in a pretty long time," Polly says. "I think it's the first I've been able to relax since the attack."

"Wait, what?" Jenna asks. "Attack? Did you say the attack?"

Mark sits up. "Attack?" He demands. "What? Who did..."

Jenna leans close to Polly, and touches her forearm. "Polly, we don't know what you're saying. If something bad happened, you never told us. We never knew."

"Obviously it was him." Mark glares at Greyson. "What did you do to her?"

Polly sighs, shaking her head, but doesn't begin to cry.

"Say it," Mark insists. "Stand up to him, say it out loud. We'll protect you."

Greyson jumps up so forcefully, his lounge tips into the water and sinks to the bottom. He glares, hair wild, ridiculous in his tiny yellow brief. He flies at Mark in a rush, a movement too sudden to make sense. Greyson's on top of Mark then beneath him, grappling, Mark's neck gripped under one arm.

"Greyson!" Polly shrieks.

Mark feels himself being turned, lifted, thrown. He tries to adjust, to regain control of his body, but can only spin helpless in mid-air, wondering if he might land in the water. He strikes hard ground with a crack, and slides across the polished concrete. The back of his head slams into something and he comes to a stop.

Jenna screams.

Mark feels disoriented, not exactly hurt but surprised and confused. He looks around, trying to orient himself. Where are they, what just happened? He's lying askew, sprawled against the top of the ladder that emerges from the water in the pool's corner.

Polly's shaking her head in shock and upset, muttering, "No, no, no." She hurries from the room, taking rapid, tiptoeing steps, without looking back.

"Polly!" Greyson shouts.

"God damn it, what's wrong with you?" Jenna demands, hyperventilating and upset almost to tears.

"What happened to Polly?" Mark shakes his head, trying to clear his vision, struggling to sit up. Everything is too bright, not just the wall and ceiling. All the world is luminous and terrible, full of pain. Things are happening among the four. He can't see what's going on, still doesn't understand what happened. "Where, where did she go?"

Mark's eyes adjust. By the time he can see and think, Jenna is glaring at Greyson, who looks down at the ground.

"She probably went to the bar," Greyson suggests. "Or maybe down to Utgard."

"Utgard?" Confused, Mark looks to Jenna, who shakes her head.

"She goes there to feel safe." Greyson exhales, as if anger and tension have left him after the spurt of violence. He crosses to where Mark is still trying to right himself, and helps him stand. "Sorry you made me, you know…"

Jenna runs over and shoves Greyson away from Mark, who almost falls again.

Greyson wobbles on the pool's edge. "Hey, come on, now," he says.

"This way you've been acting needs to stop." Jenna breathes heavily through her teeth, still angry. "If you could just stop, for one day, it could change the outcome of this. For all of us."

Greyson faces Jenna, fists on hips in a childish superhero pose, grinning broadly in defiance. "Me, stop? I don't need to stop nothing."

"I'm not telling you to worry about Mark or me. We can take care of ourselves. But Polly's having trouble, more and more lately, in case you haven't noticed. The way you behave, it's not fair to Polly."

"Fair to Polly?" Greyson asks. "How is anything in this world fair?" Greyson asks, turning to Mark in a menacing way, as if he might assault him again.

Shaking her head, Jenna grabs Mark's hand and leads him away from Greyson, toward the door.

"Let's go," Mark says, as if he might have some say in the matter. He wonders if everything's spinning out of control, as it seems to be, or if it's actually just the same as always before. "We're going. Let's go find Polly."

AN INTERLUDE

BOURBON IN LONELY TAVERN

On the stairs, climbing, Jenna makes a suggestion that doesn't seem open to debate.

"A detour," she says. "Brief, but crucial."

"That's all we ever do, detour and digress," Mark observes. "Every plan, always subject to change."

Greyson catches up from behind, breathing hard from running. Mark wants to be rid of him, but they need each other, especially if they want to find Polly. Nothing more is said about the scuffle. Jenna leads the trio, since she's the one with the plan. At the level of the Square Lounge, she veers through the door, crosses the big room and angles toward Lonely Tavern.

Mark can't remember whose turn it is to become bartender. Before the question can be debated or even raised, Jenna goes behind the bar.

The bartender grabs a bottle of bourbon off the shelf and opens the stopper. She lines up four shot glasses and pours. "I make this deal with you."

"There are three of us here," Greyson says, indicating the four glasses. "If Polly wanted one, maybe she shouldn't have…" He turns to Mark, seeming to expect agreement that no drinks are needed for anyone absent.

The bartender ignores Greyson, looking at Mark as she finishes pouring. "We make this deal. We all stop briefly for one bourbon, one at least, one at minimum. If after the first you desire no more, we'll continue as before, seeking the next thing to be sought. But so long as any person asks for another, I'll keep pouring. That's what a bartender does. She keeps pouring."

"This is a real good idea, Jenna," Greyson says, artificially friendly. He takes the shot and tosses it back. "Ah, yes, fine. Yeah. I needed this."

The bartender shakes her head, and drinks her own shot.

Mark follows suit, then raps his knuckles on the bar and points at Greyson. "Don't call her that," he warns.

The fourth shot remains untouched.

"Right, you're right." Greyson looks abashed. "Sorry, bartender, I mistook you for a friend, but I see now I don't recognize you after all. You must be new here."

"I am new here," the bartender says.

"I'll have one more, but only one," Greyson says. "Then we go find Polly."

The bartender nods, lips pursed with solemnity of purpose, and refills the three empty glasses. "Just a brief digression into philosophy and poison." Her voice is strange, deep and uneven. Something in her throat is wrong.

"Poison?" Mark asks. "I hope this is just good Kentucky bourbon, barkeep, and nothing so sinister as liquid death." He squints at the amber-brown liquor, then drinks it down.

The bartender takes her own second shot. "Whiskey is sacred because it's always safe, no matter what's in it. But the poison in question, henbane or maybe nightshade, that isn't for now. In your future, our future, is always another death."

"What are you talking about poison for?" Greyson asks, irritated. "You don't sound like yourself."

"When she says things that doesn't make any sense," Mark says, "it's just words she remembers from old books."

"What's the first thing you remember, when you came here?" the bartender asks. "What I remember is this. One of the four is expert in secret administration of poison. It only remains to be seen whether this will ever come into play."

Mark hates when people talk about things from books he hasn't read. Especially Jenna. He considers having a third drink, but stops himself from asking for it.

The bartender points to the fourth shot glass, untouched.

"One for your friend, when you find her. Somewhere out in this deep, wide world, this way or that, above or below, you might find her. You'll snatch her back from among the lost, and once she's found, you'll come back here. Here she'll find this waiting for her. If she comes."

"Earlier Polly told me something," Greyson says, a suspicious look coming over his face. "She told me she regrets so often saying things that aren't true. She gets emotional, and ends up making everyone upset over nothing."

Mark wants to know what Jenna thinks of Greyson's admission, but he can't look at her to see. She's still the bartender. "Why would she make up lies?" Mark asks Greyson. What seems more likely is that Greyson wants to cast doubt on what Polly said about someone trying to hurt her.

"To destroy all this," Greyson says. "She's trying to bring about an end."

"We don't need her help," Mark says.

The bartender tilts the bottle, trying to get their attention. "Does anyone want a last dose to speed you on your way?"

"Nah," Greyson says. "We'd better go."

"I hate to exercise after drinking." Mark says. "It makes me feel sluggish."

The bartender corks the bottle and changes her face.

Jenna steps out from behind the bar. "Didn't we already work out today? I thought we did."

"Yesterday," Greyson says.

Jenna sniffs. "I thought we already did."

"Yesterday doesn't count," Mark says. "We have to treat every day like it's separate from other days. So we always have to exercise again, even when we already have."

"Fine, fine." Jenna shrugs, fully back to herself again. She leads the men back to the stairs. "Anyway, we'll sober up before we catch Polly."

Mark has a suspicion about Greyson and Polly, a hunch about a secret. "What's on your wall?" He nudges Greyson. "What do you see every morning?"

Greyson keeps walking as if he hasn't heard, looking down at his right hand, flexing it in and out of a fist, like Polly does when she's trying to rein in her emotions.

Many times Mark has wondered whether Polly and Greyson might be going through exactly the same disconnection as himself and Jenna, not sharing one room, but residing separately at their end of the long hall.

"Why are you asking that?" Greyson asks with caution.

"In all the rooms, there's a nature image," Mark clarifies. "I'm asking about the picture in your room, the room you share with Polly."

Greyson stops, looking at Mark as if confused, then starts walking again, shaking his head. "I'm surprised you're asking. You've seen it enough times."

Mark can't recall having seen their room, or for that matter having been as far as the opposite end of the hall. He can picture it, but he's sure he hasn't been there.

"Don't you remember, dummy?" Greyson continues, seeming to sense he has Mark at a disadvantage. "When it was your room?"

Mark has no idea at all what Greyson means to suggest.

"Humor me, then," Mark says. "What do you see when you wake up beside Polly every morning?"

Greyson looks sick, almost grief-stricken at remembering. "Snow on a mountainside. A giant wolf bound in ropes, surrounded by rough men with beards, and women with braided hair. They've captured and tied the wolf, but I don't know what happens next."

This might be something Mark remembers after all. He's unsure when or where he's seen it, and can't very well ask Greyson or Jenna if he once resided in a different room, or shared someone else's bed. Now he's feeling defensive and confused, the way he wanted to make Greyson feel. He's done this to himself.

SIX

BOTTOM CAVERN, TUNNEL AND DOOR

Mark isn't sure this place they call Bottom Cavern is truly at the bottom of everything. They use the name because they're unaware of anything deeper, but it makes sense to imagine there's always something higher, and always something lower.

Where every other level feels finished, like an outcome of intentional construction followed through from design to completion, the cavern is rough, dark and damp, like a root cellar beneath an old house. Though the ceiling is high, somehow Mark always feels he should keep his head down.

The floor and walls vary from polished concrete to natural, broken stone, and back again. The stairway empties onto a concrete landing, from which the floor slopes away, crisscrossed by heavy black pipes and thin silver conduits, which sometimes turn abruptly ninety degrees and shoot upward to penetrate the ceiling, presumably conveying electricity, water or other resources above.

Mark pauses at the threshold of the landing. Jenna and Greyson go ahead and only stop when they reach a platform against the stone wall, just off-level enough to suggest the floor may be natural. There stands a heavy wood workbench, worn and chipped with use, gray with age. Beyond this stand dozens of upright oak barrels, as might hold wine. Jenna peeks into one.

"Apples." She fully removes the lid to reveal the contents. "How long have these been here?"

Mark approaches, amazed. The apples seem unnaturally red and glossy, more like the ideal conception of apples than the real thing. "They say apples can remain fresh a very long time," he speculates, though this doesn't answer Jenna's question. "At least in cool, dark places."

"Polly always talks about her apples," Greyson says. "Apples keep us young; she always says. Apples are important throughout history. Apples appear in all the old fables. Apples will keep you alive forever."

Mark takes one from the barrel, gazing at it in wonder. He can't believe it's actually what it appears to be. He takes a bite, and finds it to be a real, crisp apple, surprisingly cold and very sweet. Taste and smell provoke a rush of memories from before he became the person he is now.

"What are you saying about Polly?" Jenna asks Greyson, before taking an apple for herself.

"This bench," Greyson gestures. "She's been coming down, trying to build these fake things." He makes a disgusted face and knocks the apple from Mark's hand. It bounces under the workbench.

Mark wants another, and almost takes one, but Greyson quickly moves on past the barrels, shouting Polly's name. The next section of room, Mark can't remember having seen. The wall to their left is rugged, especially cracked and broken. A fissure opens, almost a narrow canyon, depths lost in shadow. Even within that darkness, Mark is able to see something. He strains to discern the shape, and finally recognizes it. An enormous tree root protrudes from the stone wall, reaching down from somewhere above.

"Do you see this?" Mark shouts, gently touching the root with a fingertip. He feels a vibration, something alive and shifting within the wood, almost like breathing. It makes him shiver. "Wow."

Neither Jenna nor Greyson respond. They seem not to have noticed his exclamation.

Mark can't imagine the scale of a tree large enough to extend roots so far below ground. He's read stories, myths of enormous, world-sized trees, not that such things exist in the natural world. This is a real tree, large enough to send down roots through hundreds or even thousands of feet of bedrock.

Jenna and Greyson are far ahead of him now, where the walls are once again smooth concrete, unbroken by intrusions. He hurries to catch up, pushing aside the notions that briefly filled his imagination with wonder.

As they explore deeper, farther from the entrance, the room seems more natural and cave-like. Generally, the sense of designed habitat decreases. The far wall is not visible, beyond reach of the powerful overhead lights near the entrance.

Here, to Mark's left, something else grabs his attention. A tunnel shoots off from the room's rough circle into unfinished rock. He can't help but be drawn toward the yawning, cave-like opening. This remains one of the great unknowns of this place, despite their efforts, as long as they've been here, to relentlessly explore and catalog every room, every level. Mark can imagine no reason for this unfinished tunnel to exist. It lacks any fixtures, hardware, lights, cabling or other signs of civilization found everywhere else. Though nothing of interest has ever been discovered here, Mark finds it impossible that such a way should exist, yet lead to nothing at all. If a trail is made, a road paved, a tunnel cut, that indicates somebody created it for a reason. He's always felt compelled toward this spot, even if he doesn't understand why, and feels mostly frustration at being unable to follow the tunnel very far.

Wouldn't a tunnel like this attract Polly, especially in her state of confusion?

"Don't bother," Greyson says, apparently seeing the spell being exerted upon Mark. "There's nothing down there."

Mark feels irritated at Greyson's presumption in telling him where to go. Does Greyson think he knows more? Mark's the one who possesses knowledge that he can withhold from the others, or dole out in tantalizing hints. Here, Greyson suggests otherwise. What does he think he knows?

"We should explore everywhere," Jenna says, joining Mark. "Just in case."

Greyson shrugs. "Knock yourself out." He continues on alone, still looking over his shoulder to see whether Mark and Jenna might follow.

Mark wants to explore, but also to avoid being drawn into a literal dead end. "Maybe he's right," he says with reluctance.

"We've never found anything down this passage."

"Somebody's got to come with me." Jenna gives Mark a look both imploring and frustrated. "At least take a look." She takes a few careful steps into the tunnel, mindful of the uneven floor.

"Waste of time," Greyson shouts from a distance.

"What the hell do you know?" Jenna shouts back, then whispers to Mark, as he joins her. "There's no way to see how far it extends unless we keep going."

"But haven't we been here before? It doesn't go anywhere, right?"

"It didn't before," Jenna agrees. "It's not like I think this is going to emerge on the surface, or lead down to other, new levels, but even if it leads nowhere, she could be down here, hiding in the dark. Couldn't she?"

Mark keeps close to Jenna. "That's the far wall, isn't it?" He points, indicating a wall he can't see, but imagines to be only a few feet away.

Jenna edges forward in tiny, shuffling steps, as if nearing a cliff's edge. One hand reaches into darkness, feeling for an invisible limit. She gasps, startled, then turns back, brow knit with worry. "I guess there's nothing."

"We'll find her," Greyson shouts from far off. "She always does this."

"Since when?" Jenna asks Mark, quietly.

Mark and Jenna retrace their steps to the main cavern, not eager to rejoin Greyson, but pleased to be back in familiar territory, within reach of lights.

"She always does this, all the time," Greyson sputters. "I can't even count how many times."

"No," Mark says. "Never before this. She just cries. She never runs away."

Greyson steps forcefully toward Mark, trying to intimidate. "Look who's getting sassy. You're forgetting I can do whatever I want to you." He bumps Mark, chest to chest. Mark sees him coming and leans in, but Greyson's weight knocks him back. Mark takes a step back and steadies himself, reaching the wall behind him.

"Stop, stop it." Jenna places a hand against Greyson's chest, without force.

Greyson appears to push back, but when Jenna doesn't budge, he backs off.

"What else is there to look at?" Mark asks. "It's a huge room, but there's nothing here, just cables and pipes and fixtures."

"Polly comes here because it's a place the rest of us never go," Greyson suggests.

"I come here a lot," Jenna says.

"What, when?" Mark asks, surprised. "Why?"

Greyson scoffs at the pathetic eagerness of Mark's questions.

Jenna points to the darkest corner, beyond the reach of their explorations. "The door. I keep checking, in case it opens. I can't help myself."

Mark squints, seeking for some feature or landmark he's been missing. Is there something he's forgotten? He hopes Jenna's kidding.

She looks at him, flatly surprised he doesn't understand. "The Utgard door."

Mark looks to Greyson, then back at Jenna. "Show me, then."

She leads, confident in the path, traversing obstacles, leaping barriers, ducking below hanging cables, going over, under and around horizontal and vertical pipes which range from finger-thin to broad as a tree trunk. Concrete cubes, humming steel cylinders in gleaming silver, painted white, or gone to rust. A row of giant fans spin so fast, the humming blades can be heard and felt, but not seen.

Jenna stops at an undifferentiated section of plain wall. From the rough stone emerges a handle of brushed stainless steel.

"Here." Jenna gives the handle a tug. "See? Always locked."

Above the handle is a small inscribed panel, which Mark can't stop himself from reading aloud. "Utgard."

"Right, right, that's right," Greyson says, as if grasping, then continues in a more definitive tone. "From mythology, I believe. Isn't that right? Some kind of historic significance, if you will."

"It means outyard, or outer yard," Jenna says.

"No, it doesn't," Greyson insists. "How would you even know a foreign language?"

"Stop it," Mark says, shaking his head. He's stunned to discover something like this here, after all this time. Vaguely he recalls Jenna having mentioned the word Utgard. At the time he believed it was a word he recognized, and didn't give it much thought. Now, it makes no sense. The discovery of a door in this place, with this name attached to it, comes as a shock. He tries the handle, even though he's seen Jenna pull without success.

"This door will never, ever open," she says. "We shouldn't even hope for it. Because if it does, that's the end. Somebody will have to start over."

Greyson takes his turn tugging, putting all his weight into it. He grunts and strains, even tries to gain leverage by putting a foot against the wall and heaving with his entire body.

"What was Polly saying before she ran?" Mark asks Greyson, trying to remember clues. "What did you do to her?"

"Do to her? Nothing. She got upset because I threw you around by the pool." Greyson releases the handle and shoots Mark a dismissive smirk. "She hates conflict. You know, for one thing, you could stop fucking winding me up, man."

"Let's please at least find Polly before we blow up again," Jenna pleads.

"No, she said you did something to her," Mark insists, certain the truth might explain where Polly went. "Violence, or a threat. What was she talking about?"

"Forget it, none of it's your business anyway." Greyson thumps Mark on the sternum. "Me and Polly, it's family business. Mind your own, how about that?"

Mark shoots Jenna a glance, wondering what Greyson's comment will make her think. Are Greyson and Polly married? Does Jenna think of Mark as her family, or does she know Mark thinks of her in that way? This makes him want to lash out at Greyson. "Polly gets upset, and we have to spend our days searching for her, or digging for drugs in the trash upstairs. That makes it my business, Jenna's too. And you're the one upsetting her."

Greyson's chin lowers, and his eyes shoot down, as if he may be questioning his own behavior for once. "That's just Polly."

"No," Mark persists, "that's because of how you treat her."

Greyson appears as near to introspection as he's ever allowed them to see, but then turns to Jenna while pointing at Mark. "I think he's the plant. It's him. It's been Mark this whole time."

"What?" Jenna looks to Mark as if he might explain.

"Him, this fucking company man right here," Greyson continues. "Our buddy, Mark, he's the one. The spy they planted in here to keep an eye on the rest of us."

Jenna looks back and forth, seeming even more confused. "That makes zero sense."

"An agent of the bureaucracy, a handler, or whatever. Not one of us, that's the deal. He's worse than a stranger. Polly says so. I thought she was paranoid, but she was right. She always knew."

"Stop it." Mark glares at Greyson, hard and direct, trying to stand over him, to impose himself by height alone. He knows Greyson's propensity to lashing out, knows he's stronger and has the skills to fight, but Mark needs him to stop talking before he says something that will change how Jenna thinks of him.

A rushing sound rises, along with a cool gust of air, as if a door's been thrown open in a warm house, letting in the chill of a storm outside. The temperature changes, as does the whole sense of place. This new atmosphere comes from somewhere unknown.

Greyson looks around, sensing it too.

Jenna watches Mark. What's she thinking? He wants to ask if she feels the cold, or hears the rushing air.

Her head tilts back, her eyes roll up in her head so only the white shows. "The wolf won't cry forever," Jenna says, voice high and keening. "Someday he'll climb out, he'll ride, he'll rear up and devour god. Then who'll be crying?"

Mark studies this woman, someone he knows better than anyone. She looks the same, exactly the same Jenna as before, but part of her has disappeared. The voice belongs to someone else.

"Of course we're doomed." Greyson laughs a sick, despairing laugh. "That's the whole reason why we play, until our time runs out." He shoves Mark backward, but with less force than his usual assaults.

By the time Mark regains balance, Greyson has run off toward the stairs, jumping over and ducking obstacles with surprising ease. He disappears.

Jenna gasps, as if she's just surfaced after a long underwater swim. "What was that? What just happened?"

Mark recognizes her again, not only her voice, but her eyes. This is the way she always looks at him, at once affectionate and distant. "Do you remember what you were saying?" he asks.

She shakes her head slowly, seeming confused. She starts walking and gestures for him to follow. "We'll find Jenna upstairs. I mean, Polly. We'll find Polly."

AN INTERLUDE

COMPARISON OF WISHES

They were going to look for Polly.

They were going to look for Greyson.

For some reason they're not looking. Instead, Mark is in his tiny white room, unsure how long he's been here alone.

He focuses on the antique watch. The beautiful relic he repaired himself is off his wrist, resting in his palm. It terrifies him to wonder what he'd do if the watch stopped working. Times like this, he wishes he had his tools.

This is where he retreats, more and more often. He excuses himself, ignoring Greyson's mockery, when stress or fear overwhelm him. Is that what he's feeling, fear, or is it obsession with Jenna? She's with him almost constantly, yet somehow they're drifting apart.

He hears a sound, someone else shifting very close by. He's not alone. She's here, Jenna is, standing right behind him. Not speaking, only watching. It's not that she's just entered. She's been here all along, and he's forgotten. It's as if Mark is lately paying less attention to the Jenna who's actually present, and instead daydreams about some invented version. That other woman is the one he wants.

"It has been stressful," Mark says, agreeing with a statement she hasn't actually voiced. "All this arguing. And searching." He glances back, looks at her directly. It's definitely her, same as before. Jenna is here with him, in his room.

He's been meaning to ask something, and almost starts to speak before he remembers he's not really sure what it was. The urgent thing he needed to know seemed so near the tip of his tongue, and only fled in the instant before he resolved to ask.

Then, the very moment he decides not to ask, he remembers what it was. He wanted to ask about the mural in her room. What piece of the world does she look at each morning when she wakes? He's afraid he's seen it before, or she's described it to him, and that it'll be embarrassing not to remember.

"I feel the same," Jenna says.

Mark's mind rushes ahead with this idea she's just stated. She feels the same.

She thinks of me all the time.

She aches for what we've lost.

She can't understand how we've fallen apart.

She wonders when we'll come back together.

This is all she ever thinks about.

"Stressed from so much conflict," she clarifies, and shows him her shaking hand. "Always trembling lately. So on edge."

"What's that game you like to play?" Mark asks. As soon as he's spoken, he wonders, did she ever really have a game, or was he thinking of Polly? Which of them is the one that loves the guessing game?

"Wishes." Jenna smiles, vaguely pleased, yet still distant.

"Do you have any wishes?" Mark wants to push onward, feeling pathetic, knowing the reason this game excites him is only the unlikely possibility she might surprise him by revealing her own wishes to coincide with his own.

He wants his tools, his clocks, his watches. All the parts survive forever, even if they stop functioning properly together. The size of a second or a year never changes. Increments accumulate, and no matter how many are added, how long it takes, each measure remains exactly the same size.

They are two people thinking different thoughts, describing different ideas, using words so vague and elliptical, so built upon wishes and dreams and half-memories, he's able to shape what she says into any form he might desire. The only way it fails is if he lets himself think about it.

"Where do you wish you lived?" Jenna asks. It's as if she's reached down into the darkness of his confusion and given him a hand to lift him back into clarity.

Mark tries to remember. "A cabin by a lake." He restrains himself from saying more. He doesn't want her to figure out what he's really thinking, which is that he only wishes she would stay here with him in this room, and share it again.

"The next time you see water," Jenna says, voice quavering so the words convey an ominous, warning quality, "it won't be a peaceful lake. It'll be a giant wave, enough to cover all the world and all time, and wash away every single yesterday."

Mark isn't sure how to respond. It always comes down to this same talk, with them. He wants to mention a new beginning. She returns to the end. Maybe they're the same.

Jenna's expression changes. She regards Mark with old, comfortable familiarity. There's intimacy in the way she leans in, lets him see her resignation. "No point in wishing, other than to make yourself feel better, if only for a second," she says.

Mark wants to disagree, but can't speak against her.

"The thing to do is forget," Jenna says. "Keep going as if you never knew anything, never even wanted anything."

Mark wants many things. He wants to change her words so they say something else. He wants her to be the kind of person he's always thinking of. Someone different.

SEVEN

GYMNASIUM, TELEVISION

Mark changes into workout clothes while Jenna waits outside. When they reach the stairs, Mark tells her what he expects.

"I'm going to think of how I would act if Polly had never screamed and run away, if Greyson had never gone crazy and attacked me and run away. Imagine if we went to the Gymnasium, and those things had never happened. That's how I'm going to act."

What would that day be like? Today is that day. He forgets the other time, when different things started to happen. This is new.

When they reach the Gymnasium, it's the version Mark has tried to imagine. Both Greyson and Polly are spinning on exercise cycles, looking at a wall-mounted television, though the screen is black and there's no sound. Their faces are neutral, neither Greyson's rage nor Polly's anxiety in evidence.

Let's pretend none of it ever happened, Mark wants to say. He doesn't actually have to speak. They already know. He can see.

Jenna drapes her towel over the rail of her preferred treadmill, the one she uses ten or twelve times a week. "You had us pretty worried," she says, addressing nobody specific.

"Everything's fine," Polly says between huffing breaths. She's pedaling fast, rocking side to side with effort. Her face is pink. Sweat dampens her hair.

"Everything's good." Greyson's sweating too. He grips the handlebars so hard, veins stand out in his forearms.

"You used the word attack," Jenna says, addressing Polly but looking at Greyson.

"Come on, nobody said that," Greyson complains.

Jenna dismounts her treadmill and stands between Polly and Greyson, breaking their line of sight. "Polly, it's what you said."

"No." Polly stops spinning and removes her glasses. She rubs the bridge of her nose, then both eyes. "What are you guys, detectives? We have to go on living here, until we don't. If you and Mark would start working, we could get enough calorie burn to run the TV for at least one show."

Jenna climbs back aboard the treadmill and presses the start button. A whirring sound rises as the motor accelerates. Three miles per hour, four, five, six. She raises the incline to six degrees. Her preferred setting, six and six.

Mark settles into the rowing machine, grips the handles and begins pulling. His back tightens, a stiffness he knows will loosen as his muscles warm. He tunes out distractions and focuses on rhythmic movement.

The TV screen blinks white, then displays a blue and gold soundstage, a game show with three players standing behind podiums displaying dollar amounts.

"Oh, fuck yes," Greyson shouts. "Here we go."

Though it's an episode they've seen many times, Greyson acts like it's new. He always does. The loop of recorded TV includes episodes of many different programs, but over time, the same shows repeat.

"What is Kepler's Second Law?" Greyson shouts at the TV, then exclaims in unison with the host, "That's correct!"

This sequence of answers and questions continues. Greyson is the only one playing.

"Who is Lauren Bacall? Correct!"

Why try to escape, or hide? Eventually the experiment will be over. Investigators will come, and we'll all try to describe what happened. Nobody's getting away with anything. Nobody escapes a full accounting.

"What the fuck are you going on about?" Greyson shouts, glaring at Mark.

Mark looks around. The others are all are looking at him. "What? Who?"

"Do you hear yourself with that bullshit, interrupting my show?" Greyson continues. "I'm talking to you, dummy. What's all that bullshit about nobody escapes?"

"Did I say something out loud?" Mark asks.

Polly rolls her eyes. "You're a fucking mess, Mark. I thought I was bad."

Greyson makes his usual scoffing laugh.

Mark wants to give in to flaring anger, but experience has taught him escalation is dangerous with Greyson. Better let it pass, be the bigger man, and his aggression will subside.

Following these thoughts, he briefly worries he might have made the same mistake again, and spoken aloud his latest stream of consciousness, but nobody looks at him now. Greyson's focus remains on the television.

Everyone's back to normal. Greyson and Polly on stationary bikes, Jenna padding lightly on the treadmill, Mark low to the ground, sliding on a rail, pulling cables attached to a spinning flywheel.

Mark's ears pop, so sharp and loud he's sure others must've heard it. Pain stabs the center of his skull. He tries to tune it out, but at the point of greatest effort in each stroke on the rower, something inside his head gives, like a valve popping open. He often wonders if there's a problem with pressurization in this place.

"My ears," Mark says, blinking, trying to look around, though he can barely open his eyes. "Anyone else?"

No answer.

"The physics don't make sense," Mark says, and stops pulling. "The cavern is lower, it's deeper than this, but my ears never pop down there."

The television flickers and goes dark, though the sound continues. When the collective calorie burn on the exercise machines drops below a certain level, first the image cuts out, then eventually the sound too. There's plenty of electricity to power the television, but this arrangement gives them incentive to exercise at high intensity, all together.

"Come on, you fucker!" Greyson shouts, banging on the

handlebar. "Get going, start pumping it, you bitch! This is important."

"Sorry, Greyson," Polly says.

"It's not your fault," Greyson says. "It's mister sensitive over there. Quit jacking off and pull that rower. For fuck's sake, it's almost the final question."

"Lighten up, Greyson," Polly says. "Jesus, you're relentless with your shittiness lately."

"So hostile," Jenna says between breaths, synchronized with her strides.

"None of this matters," Mark mutters, barely mindful of the need to row. All he's thinking about is a way past the pain.

"It does matter," Greyson insists. "Final Jeopardy is a culmination of all the promise of regular Jeopardy, multiplied by Double Jeopardy."

"It doesn't matter," Mark says, pulling again, trying to breathe, "because we've seen this episode. We've seen them all. That's why you know the answers. We all know them. You're the only one so desperately insecure, you pretend you know the answers because you're a genius, and not because we've seen every episode a thousand times."

The television screen lights up with a return of garish colors, a drug for the eyes.

"Not answers, dumbfuck," Greyson says. "Questions."

"Let him have it, Mark," Jenna says. "It hurts no one."

"Maybe you've seen it before," Greyson says. "I haven't. When I get them right, it's because I know the answers."

"Not answers, dumbfuck," Mark says. "Questions."

Polly giggles, then covers her mouth to stifle herself.

"Whoever won the prize," Jenna says, "they long ago spent their prize money and probably died. Only we're still here, watching them try to win, over and over forever. One wins, the rest lose, and we just spin and spin and spin."

"You're spinning, not me," Greyson says, spinning.

Mark pulls harder, recruiting muscles all down his back, from forearms to shoulders, hips, thighs, knees and calves. He concentrates, pulls the handle attached to the cable which turns the flywheel faster, faster. The movement blurs. It could be motionless; the stainless-steel disc is without markings to show its rotation. Heat builds in his core and radiates from his flesh into the room, becoming part of the air they all breathe. This heat has nowhere else to go.

MICHAEL GRIFFIN

AN INTERLUDE

GUESSING GAME

On the stairs, Polly wants to play a game.

"We're already playing one," Mark says. "Every day, the game of up and down stairs."

"Every time Jenna suggests a game, we always play," Polly complains. "But when I make up a game, nobody wants to play."

What Polly is saying is true. Between obligations, Jenna often suggests games she's invented to make the time pass more quickly. Mark once considered it an added benefit that the games helped them learn more about one another, but he no longer considers familiarity to be a good thing. Almost everyone treats strangers with more respect than the people they know best.

The problem is that Polly's games aren't really games, just excuses to make everyone think about Polly and talk about her. Mark hesitates to say so, but Greyson gladly does.

"Polly, you always suggest stupid games."

"Won't somebody?" Polly whines.

"Not unless you say what it is first," Jenna says, apparently thinking along the same lines as Mark and Greyson.

"Somebody else, please?" Polly's voice reaches still higher into shrillness.

Mark's the only one who hasn't refused yet. "It doesn't seem like a great idea right now," he says. "We're trying to stay calm, and not fight for a second or two. Maybe later."

"Maybe later doesn't mean you actually might play," Polly complains. "It means, shut up, Polly. It means, your ideas are terrible, Polly. It means, you're a stupid bitch, Polly."

"It doesn't mean that," Mark says.

Polly rallies, starting over with fresh enthusiasm, as if suggesting the game for the first time. "Come on, you guys! If we all play, it won't take as long. Everybody, three guesses each. Or five."

At the next landing, Greyson surprises everyone by agreeing. "Okay, Polly. What kind of guesses?"

"You know, you know." Polly claps her hands rapidly and squeaks in a way that means she's happy. "The game of guess what Polly's thinking of. Who goes first? Mark, you go first!"

"Okay," Mark concedes, because he seems not to have any choice. He concentrates on receiving a clear mental vision of whatever Polly's thinking of.

"I'll guess," Jenna says. "You're thinking of that time detectives found Greyson's cut-up body stashed under Mark's bed."

Greyson gives Polly a look, which Mark interprets to mean, *Did you notice what Jenna just said? Not 'our bed,' but 'Mark's bed.'* But if that's what they're thinking, neither says anything. Maybe they already know, and only wonder why Mark and Jenna keep pretending.

"I never think negative things," Polly says. "Mark, you first. It's your turn."

Mark tries to recall her story. "You're thinking of the time when you were thirteen, a salesman knocked on your front door, and you answered, and the man forced his way in and kissed you."

"No," Polly says. "That's close, but no."

"You're thinking of animal cookies sprinkled with blue sugar, with hot cinnamon candies for eyes," Greyson says.

"Yes, yes, good guess!" Polly claps her hands. "Godzilla cookies, like our mom made."

"Whose mom?" Mark asks.

"Ours, dummy," Greyson says. "Polly's and mine. Duh."

"Wait, what?" Mark asks, disbelieving. "Both of you, the same mom?"

"Same mom, same dad," Polly says flatly.

Mark turns to Jenna. "Did you know about this?"

Jenna shakes her head, confused. "You two… are brother and sister?"

"We've only mentioned it like a thousand times," Greyson says. "We're twins, obviously. I mean, we're both artists. Also, did you not notice we look exactly alike?"

Mark can't believe he's missed something so important. Jenna too is surprised, but there's no way Greyson or Polly has ever mentioned this before. What's more, Mark's absolutely certain he's seen them being physically demonstrative, not just affectionate in a brother-sister way, but intimate. They've talked at times about each other's relatives, not a single shared family. He's about to press for clarification when Polly stops walking and falls behind.

When the others notice and turn back, Polly begins acting strangely. She bends forward at the waist and straightens, bends and straightens again and again, like some strange, repetitive exercise. Her mouth hangs open and her eyes widen, evoking innocent surprise, rather than fear.

It's not only her movements, but her features and color. Her hair hangs straight, no longer kinky. Skin smooth, unmarked by any hint of the freckles she hates. Eyes clear and steady, as if she's shed her usual worry.

Greyson turns away and resumes walking. Jenna follows, then before Mark can approach to check on her, Polly shrugs off the grossest of involuntary movements. She straightens and follows the others, still looking changed, not quite the same Polly who began the day.

"This can't continue," Mark mutters. What most worries him is the possibility that it might.

EIGHT

MARBLE MUSEUM WITH BLAST DOOR

Time proceeds, seconds spinning, days piling up to become a teetering monument of years. Spaces accumulate vertically, levels stacked like layer cake. If some day there arrives a cutoff point after which all time ceases, at least finally there will be a stop to the endless seeking, climbing and descending.

Mark worries that after being so distracted by internal wishes and hopes, he might miss external signs when they come.

And now, there's something new, a sign of change. A sound.

"Shh, shh." Mark stops, holds himself critically still, listening for something he may have heard. There is no clue to help clarify what may have happened, yet he's certain. "Something's different. Something opened."

Polly's eyes widen, more excited by Mark's reaction than anything she's noticed herself. "Maybe you're right this time!"

Jenna's brow furrows, more in fear than excitement. "I feel something too."

Greyson nods, as dreadful possibilities seems to dawn. "What is it? Someone coming?"

"Did you hear that sound?" Polly whispers with nervous intensity. Both hands fly to her face, eyes wide. "What does it mean? What's going to happen, Mark?"

"Don't be scared," Greyson assures her. "It'll be okay."

"What is it?" Jenna asks. "Where should we go? Where haven't we looked yet?"

Mark tries to remember. "We never finished searching Bottom Cavern."

"We looked there for Polly," Greyson says. "But she's here now, we found her. There's no reason to go down again."

Mark remains convinced exploration is in order. The only place they've visited less frequently than Bottom Cavern is the opposite extreme, the uppermost entry chamber they call the Marble Museum. Why have they stopped going there? Probably because the blast door clarifies the reality of being sealed in. Confinement is hard enough without facing the constant reminder of lacking control over whether or not they'll ever be able to leave.

"I don't know what we're looking for," Mark says cautiously, "but I've always felt that we'll discover whatever we need to know."

"Something really has opened up," Jenna says. "Hasn't it?"

"Maybe it's the end." Polly trembles visibly. "We should go up. I mean, we're already climbing. Let's keep going, all the way."

"Maybe it's open," Jenna says, breathless. "The door, could it be open?"

"It could." Greyson's expression mingles wonder and fright. "Maybe it unlatched and swung open, and we could walk up and out into the world any time we want."

"Oh my god," Jenna says. "Oh, wow."

Mark surges ahead and leads the way. He climbs fast, energized, mindless of his fatigue, unaware how hard he's breathing. Every landing and doorway passes in a blur until the top.

"This one is strange," Jenna says, and steps into the top level. "So strange."

Each level has a purpose, but Marble Museum offers unusual contradictions. The exit wall is dominated by a steel blast door supported by massive hydraulic arms, while most of the room is a gleaming white stone gallery full of sumptuous paintings and classical sculptures. Stairs curve up along the outer wall to a broad circular catwalk that overlooks the chamber. At the room's center, the trunk of a giant ash tree emerges from the marble floor and rises to penetrate the ceiling, roots hidden somewhere below, branches and leaves presumably above. No other signs of this tree or any other can be seen in any level other than this one, and Bottom Cavern.

Mark has always liked to imagine the tree has somehow found the surface, penetrating earth and stone to reach open air and sunlight. How else could it continue to grow and thrive? If it were dead, it would soften and rot.

One thing he remembers from this room is the way his ears popped when the massive hinges pulled shut the drive-over blast door. It tilted up to vertical and settled into machined grooves, sealing out the world. That sense of pressure is all he recalls of what must have been the time of his arrival. He remembers none of the others being present.

As they reach a point far enough into the room to see past the stone pillars and statues, they all stop at once. No one breathes.

Despite everyone's hopes, the door remains shut.

"Oh, no," Jenna moans.

"Damn it, just…" Polly sputters, breaking the silence. "God damn it!"

"It felt like something was different," Mark says, wondering if that's really the way it felt, or if he only ever experienced wishful thinking. "I guess it isn't time."

"As if there's ever going to be any right time," Jenna says, with uncharacteristic frustration. "Or any purpose to any part of this."

"There's always purpose," Polly says, trying to seem like she really means it.

"We ignore time passing," Jenna says, "so it carries us faster, faster. Dangerously fast."

"What do you suppose the weather's like outside?" Polly asks, looking up.

It's treacherous up there, Mark wants to say. It always has been.

Jenna places a hand against the blast door and pushes, as if this small added pressure might cause the solidly anchored metal to flatten and open inward. She turns to face the others. "We can't feel it, or see it, but the world's still moving. The winds, the tides."

Mark thinks of the wind, and realizes the air is definitely still moving. He felt it before, and still feels it, even though they've ruled out that it's coming from this level.

"This," Mark begins slowly, cautiously, "is what I think."

"Yes, tell." Polly seems eager to hear.

"The test is to prove being hidden from sun, from rain, from fresh air, from radiation, from media and human interaction, won't protect us from changing."

"Changing?" Greyson asks.

"Yes," Mark says. "I don't remember what it's called, the big event, that one that has a long name. An important word, one that's on the tip of my tongue. You know what I mean, you remember before. The end of things. Broken memories, shifted consciousness, misplaced emotions. Inappropriate love and desire. Our lives feel like they're moving too fast, and it's because they're constantly on the verge of ending at any moment."

Greyson scowls. "Come on, you're just making shit up."

"You talk about it like it's a story we're all supposed to know," Polly says.

"Yes, we should. From all the times it's happened before." Mark wants to project more confidence than he feels.

Greyson approaches, grips Mark firmly by the shoulders and starts pushing him backward. This time he's not trying to shove him down, only to move him back a few steps until he stops against a statue of a slim, naked youth holding a spear.

"You can't tell us now, after all this time, you've always known what this is." Greyson's usual hostility has shifted to an angular terseness born of fear. "Why do we keep waking up here, keep going through these motions, unless that's what life is supposed to be?"

"Stop it, both of you!" Polly shrieks. Her face reddens and tears well in her eyes.

Mark removes Greyson's hands from his shoulders, and Greyson doesn't resist. This restraint is somehow more disconcerting than his usual aggression. Mark doesn't know what to say. Admit he doesn't know, that he only said those things because he wants to feel there's some point to this? If he pretends he knows, the others might listen. Everybody wants to believe what they're doing has some kind of meaning.

Mark could stop talking, go back to his room, but instead he elaborates. "The impasse is this: Humankind's innate nature is destructive to the very human project."

"What are you talking about?" Jenna asks. "Just the usual bickering?"

"No, more than that," Mark says. "Our real stories are all murder, incest, betrayal—"

"Stop throwing around words," Greyson says.

"You hate hearing those words because you're the cause," Mark says.

"He's right," Jenna agrees. "Polly's afraid to tell. You make her afraid."

"Bullshit."

"Stop it!" Polly cries, a jagged shriek.

The ground rumbles, the walls shake.

Jenna looks around. "This might be it."

The air moves, a rushing wind.

"So what do you think, why is there a museum here?" Greyson asks, gesturing.

"He asked, trying to change the subject," Jenna says.

"What are they trying to tell us?" Greyson continues.

"This door may not be open," Mark says, indicating the blast door, "but another is, somewhere. Air from outside's getting in."

Jenna steps closer to Mark. "Where?"

Greyson staggers away from the others, fingers splayed wide.

Mark ignores him. "It has to be all the way down."

Greyson's mouth contorts as if stifling a scream, and his head shakes and bobs, with the occasional hard snap to the left.

"What's he trying to say?" Polly approaches Greyson, but stays out of reach.

Greyson's mouth opens in a silent scream. His bulging eyes redden and watery tears fall. His skin whitens, becomes wrinkled; his face and neck splits and tears like crepe paper, but without bleeding.

"I don't need this," Jenna says, backing away. "I don't. I'm a married woman with two beautiful girls. I don't want any more drama. I only want to get through this and get back to my family."

Jenna's words steal Mark's attention from whatever's happening to Greyson. What did she say?

Married.

What does that mean? Himself and Jenna, was that only an affair, was she only ever pretending she wanted him, loved him? If this has always been her situation, how can he never have seen? He used to lie beside her, watch her so closely, listen as she slept. Her skin, her breathing beneath his gentle touch. He's never really known Jenna.

"Married." He tries to laugh. "You're not married. You don't have kids."

He looks to Greyson, who can't even hold himself together, let alone help Mark understand. Greyson falls to the floor, body crumpling in on itself, bones folding into inhuman angles. It's like when Polly transformed earlier, but more profound. Now Polly stands over him, but doesn't dare touch.

What words can Mark say to Jenna? Nothing. It's too late to pretend this hasn't destroyed him. He turns, leaving the others behind, and walks for the stairs. After a few steps, he can't stop himself from running.

AN INTERLUDE

WEDDING DRESS
AND HIDDEN GUN

In his room, Mark obsesses on the ticking of his watch. The passing of time is impossible to prevent, but Mark wishes he could disassemble and reassemble the parts so the days would pass the way they're supposed to. He lacks the tools. In this place, he's made do with only this one watch, and no means to keep it working the way he wants.

The ticking sounds correct, steady and clear. The interval of time between every tick is exactly the same length. The problem is, the gaps are the wrong size. He laments that he can't fix things any more. It's sad, the way life has become a hurried, meaningless rush, without satisfaction.

There's a knock on the door. Before he can think who it might be, let alone stand and answer, the door opens. It's Jenna.

"Sorry," Mark says. "Had to gather myself."

"I know," Jenna says. "I feel the same. We keep breaking and transforming, one at a time. I'm next, then you."

"I always think the problem is just Greyson," Mark says, fussing with the watch to no effect. "Maybe it's all of us."

Jenna turns and kneels by the clothing box at the foot of the bed. She touches the lid, and glances at Mark. "Polly's staying with Greyson, until he's back to normal. They'll wait for us. You're right, we need to keep looking. See where the wind's getting in."

She opens the lid and Mark panics, certain she'll find the hidden gun and bullets. He can't think what he could say to stop her, or how to explain, should she find them.

"Wait," he whispers.

Jenna reaches past Mark's clothes toward the bottom, as if she knows what's hidden.

There's nothing he can say, no way to stop her. Not without admitting what he's hidden, and having to explain what he wants to happen.

Jenna glances at him, smiling without concern, feeling around beneath his stacked clothing as if certain she'll find what she seeks. "There's no avoiding that it's four of us, beginning to end. That's how it's got to be, love it or hate it. Four, or none. We separate and come back together, over and over again."

What she comes up with is not the gun or bullets, but a white cardboard gift box, too large to have fit inside the locker. Mark's certain it wasn't in there before.

Jenna lifts the lid to reveal a wedding dress, cream lace and ornament, or maybe white gone dingy with age. "Most of my life, I kept this beneath my bed." She stands and holds out the dress before her so it hangs straight. The size of the dress suits the thinness she only recently achieved.

"Jenna," he says.

"It's antique, full of holes." Her voice breaks and tears form in the corners of her eyes. "But there's nothing else like it."

It's not only colored with age, but falling apart, so ragged and threadbare it probably wouldn't hold together if worn.

"It's the only one to be found," Jenna says.

"Is someone having a wedding?" Mark asks.

"Remember what you always told me?" she asks.

Mark tries to remember, struggling to come up with good, convincing words that might fix this. He can't. He has nothing.

"That when it's time, we'll know. When the end comes, it'll be obvious. A giant wave looming on the horizon."

"I said that?"

Jenna nods. "A line will mark the end of a cycle. After, there's no more future, but also, no more doubt. No way of going back. You await the end. You open your eyes and face it when it comes."

He tries to remember using these words, but doesn't even recognize the ideas they express. "What do I mean?"

Jenna drapes the dress over the edge of his bed. "This is what it comes down to. Either the wolf has to die, or we do."

The wolf is another thing everyone's been mentioning lately. Wolf is a word they all keep saying, but without understanding what it means.

The wristwatch ticks. Mark watches Jenna begin to transform. Her hair is shorter and uneven, as if hacked away in anger with a blunt knife. She wears the dress, not only old and frayed, but muddy and wet where the hem trails on the ground, stuck through with pine needles. Her belly is swollen, arms held out to her sides.

"This isn't the first time," Jenna says, overcome with sadness and regret. "I've told you before. I keep telling you."

"And I'm sorry," Mark says, apologizing because he doesn't remember, doesn't even know what she means. He wishes he didn't have to disappoint Jenna.

She's transformed so much, how can he look at her and not say something? Of course she knows. She must know.

"Don't be sorry." Jenna smiles sadly. "Anyway, if it happens again, you won't remember this. Probably I won't either."

Mark has an idea, a possible solution. "Maybe it's time we all go watch the videos for instructions. Aren't there supposed to be films or something?" As soon as he says this, he doubts it. "Am I wrong? Isn't there a rule that if we can't continue, we find a message that tells us what to do next?"

"That's not true, is it?" she asks, then seems to second guess herself. "It must be written somewhere. Does anyone have the documents?"

Mark looks around his room, as if he might find instructions sitting out in some obvious place. He shakes his head. "What about the others? Where are Polly and Greyson?"

"Outside." Jenna seems relieved to have been asked something she's sure of. "Polly said they'd wait in the stairs, while Greyson calms down. We'll all go down together."

"OK, you go ahead," Mark says. "I'll be right there, two seconds behind."

Jenna looks distracted. Her hand drifts to her belly. She appears shocked to find it's flat again, like it always used to be.

The wedding dress is draped across the bed.

"We'll go down, then." Looking confused as to why Mark isn't following, she opens the door, goes outside and closes it behind her.

Trying not to make a sound, Mark reopens the metal box. He finds the gun, loads the four bullets, then puts the weapon in his back pocket and untucks his shirt to conceal it.

NINE

FOR EACH THEIR OWN MESSAGE

In the stairwell echo chamber, cool wind rushes. Mark hurries down, trying to catch the others. Part of him believes there's no chance they'll escape without him. A small, fearful voice says, *don't end up left here all alone.*

With each level he descends, the chill grows more pronounced. At bottom, in addition to the whoosh of breeze, another sound rises to the level of notice. A deep, vibrating hum.

"Does anybody hear that?" Mark asks, though he's still alone.

Something is changing, no question.

Mark emerges from the stairs, crosses the landing and descends into the wide openness of Bottom Cavern.

Not far off, he sees the others and jogs toward them. Jenna faces the Utgard door, now standing open, one hand gripping the outer edge. Polly and Greyson crowd behind her, all three looking into whatever lies beyond the threshold.

The cavern room swirls with outdoor air, as if past the door must lie a forest, a scrim of trees, a clear blue lake. The outer world has found this place. Real nature, not just a picture.

It's the end of everything. The start of the new.

Mark reaches the others, and sees what they see. It's not the nature vista he expects. Beyond the door is a narrow room, barely more than a short hallway. On wood tables, left and right, stand electronic components mounted in racks, like a radio studio from a bygone era. On either side of both tables are closed doors, four in all.

"This must be where," Polly whispers.

Jenna turns at Mark's approach. "You go ahead," she urges him.

"You're the one who's going to know. You can explain to the rest of us."

Mark moves past, eyeing each of the inner doors in turn. "They're identical. One for each." His hand finds the latch of the rearmost door on the right.

A voice behind him speaks. "Before you go see, sprinkle dust in your eyes."

Without looking back, he opens the door and finds yet another smaller room, barely more than a closet. On a wood desk rests a television or computer display that looks like it's been assembled from mismatched parts. The smell is stale, dusty, with a hint of ozone. Before the table is a stool.

The door swings shut behind him. The lock clicks. Mark tries the handle, which moves freely, but the door won't budge. A dead-bolt must've slipped into place. A trap, Mark laughs. A trap within a trap.

He searches for any means of unlocking the bolt, but whatever controls it must be electronic rather than mechanical. Wires run from the door's metal frame up the front wall to the ceiling, then down the back wall to the desk where they connect to exposed circuit boards in the base of the display.

It occurs to him, or possibly he remembers, that the door should open automatically, like how it locked. This should happen after he sees what he's meant to see. Maybe the instructions are here. Didn't he just tell Jenna each of them would find what they needed to know, at the right time?

It's time now.

The screen flashes to brightness, like the Gymnasium TV illuminated when all four exercised together. This picture isn't game shows, but something more abstract. Forms emerge out of grey static. Dark vertical lines in the foreground overlap two horizontal halves. The narrow lines are trees, moving slightly, swaying in a wind. The horizon divides sky and water. The static makes a sound, though no speakers are apparent.

He wants to close his eyes, to avoid seeing. But isn't this what he's always wanted, to learn what he doesn't know, to be able to see beyond, and maybe finally understand?

Mark sits on the stool, staring into the screen. He can't help wondering what the others are experiencing. Are they waiting outside for him to finish, or already locked away within their own rooms, seeing messages on their own screens?

Behind static, a monotone voice speaks letters and numbers in patterns, like a code.

"I'm ready," Mark says.

After a pause, questions begin, but he's too preoccupied to pay attention at first. When he doesn't answer the first, others follow. Several pass before Mark decides to listen and to answer. He has no idea if anyone can see him, or hear his responses. He doesn't know who it is that's asking.

"Do you remember, what do you think is your name?" The voice is strange.

"My name is Mark."

"Do you know, what is the number of the year?"

"This year," he says, intending this as an answer.

"Can you guess, what is in my mind I'm thinking of?"

He recalls Polly's games, and Jenna's, and role-playing in Lonely Tavern. Is one of the women trying to make him guess? The voice isn't Jenna's or Polly's. Maybe the others are outside, somehow asking the questions in another voice, and watching his responses.

Mark used to believe he was never quite lost, just disoriented, or sometimes confused. Walking through morning rituals, recurrent meals, a cycle of enforced exercise and dosing with strange medicines, all these actions seemed to arise from his own choices. Not automatic, never compulsory.

The image wavers, overlaid with a face. The eyes resemble his own, but not the way his eyes really look. The way he imagines his eyes.

The mouth moves, forming words.

"There's nothing after this," someone says. "After, everything stops."

Wind rushes, only a sound. The screen flickers, dark, then back to light.

Now the face superimposed over forest and lake disappears. One brief scene after another plays out, narratives depicting people alone or in groups of two, three or four. Many such scenarios pass before he realizes these are his friends, the only people he knows. They're familiar, he recognizes them, but they're also different somehow. More like costumed actors portraying real people based on secondhand descriptions of appearance and manner.

Greyson, or a taller version of him with a great red beard, straddles a crack in the earth, wrestling a giant serpent. The coil wraps around his body, seeming to crush him.

Jenna and Polly fight each other with knives. Many cuts, much blood streaming to the ground. Their moves become slow, both dying. They are sisters.

Mark himself, slipping barefoot on a snowy mountain slope, trying to fight a wolf, much larger than himself. The wolf tears chunks from his flesh. The wounds are bloodless, but he appears to weaken and falls.

The world flips, darkens, shifts.

The wolf looms, mouth widens, devours him whole.

A change of perspective. All light is sealed away, outside, then it intrudes again. Powerful hands pull open the wolf's jaws. Someone grasps Mark and pulls him out, whole and gasping, into freezing air. A pale-skinned form, moving fast and with great force, pulls the jaws wider until bones fracture. Another jerk and the wolf's neck is broken. It falls, lies motionless. With a long, needle-like spear, the pale figure pins the dying wolf to the ground. Mark looks on, gasping, bleeding.

Standing over him, holding the needle that kills the wolf, is a man whose eyes are very old though his naked body is youthful, slim and hairless.

From behind him steps a woman, similarly pale and unblemished. Like the man, she appears young in body, while conveying a sense of having watched many ages pass. Her hair is striking, white and long and very straight. Her breasts have no nipples, her eyes no lashes.

When the young man turns, Mark sees he too lacks nipples and eyelashes. Both bodies resemble glossy, polished stone. Mark recalls twin sculptures in the Marble Museum, a man and woman who seemed to watch over the room. These two are the same.

How long have these twin ideals of sculptural form, seeming objects to be viewed and admired, in fact been watching, waiting for the arrival of their eternal moment? How many times has Mark regarded them without seeing what existed before his eyes? Always his mind makes himself the subject, makes him the actor who flashes his vision and scrutiny onto the world, planning actions, offering judgment. The truth is, he has always required explanation before he could understand, always needed a trigger from outside himself.

"No more being born, no more dying," the woman says, in a familiar voice, addressing the Mark who's watching the screen, not the Mark pulled from the wolf's belly. "A storm turns. Run now, climb up, out. Go to a new world."

The slim man must be her twin. "The world is new," he says.

Are the others seeing this same thing, or something of their own?

"I'll guess what you were thinking," Mark says, knowing his answer to the final question comes too late. "You thought of a time before we arrived."

The image freezes. Twins inhumanly perfect, a dying wolf, Mark's blood-smeared actor hyperventilating in the snow. He presses knuckles into his eyes, trying to eradicate the sights. He thought it would be better to know.

"Better to wonder," he says, watching the screen.

The picture doesn't move, but new words rush, too fast to understand.

"Who's speaking?" Mark asks. "Is anyone listening? I hear. Can you hear me?"

A flurry of voices, all at once. He's overwhelmed by overlapping word-sounds, a hundred conversations superimposed.

"Say again," Mark says. "I can't translate."

The number of voices begins to diminish, a riotous crowd, an unruly classroom, a spirited dinner party, then only a few, two, finally one. Before any meaning can be decoded or deduced, it all stops.

His frustration at being unable to comprehend is replaced by fear. All he wants is to know what he's supposed to do here, and maybe reclaim some degree of closeness with Jenna. He doesn't need perfect happiness, he's willing to work, to deal with conflicts, to have less than everything he desires, so long as the bargain is a balanced one, a net positive. But he fears he'll never be with Jenna, and no amount of obsessing or wanting will make any difference. She's drifting or pulling away, out of reach.

The screen flickers, light without shape. None of the images make sense. He's afraid all the messages are over, without any clarity granted. The screen will go dark, the door will unlock and he'll have no choice but to return to before.

"What if they're outside, waiting?" Mark whispers. "Hoping for me to explain?"

What if they've changed so much, we don't recognize each other? The possibility disturbs him.

He stands, one eye still on the screen, and glances at the door.

"I'll go out and find them coming out of their rooms at the same moment. Same as before, Jenna, Polly and Greyson." He says their names, proving he remembers.

There's another possibility. He reaches behind, finds the gun in his pocket. His hands tremble, contemplating this idea. A heartbeat pounds in his ears, synchronized with pulsing light from the monitor.

Without the gun, he might consider other options. With it, he knows what he has to do.

"I know the end can only ever be this," a voice says.

He wants to wake with a new, blank mind, to face another day unlike all the others. No hard choices. A day fresh and empty, ready to be filled.

"There was never anything left," a voice says.

"What happens when I open the door?" Mark demands, moving closer to it.

No answer. The screen is dark.

He touches the door handle, not trying to turn it, but lightly grasping, preparing himself for the possibility of trying to go out.

One hand disables the pistol's safety, the other prepares to open the door.

"Talk me out of ending this," he says.

A woman's voice answers. "This is what life is. Race in fear of being left behind, fight without reason, try to build events into a story that makes sense. These events don't connect. These days have no meaning."

"But—" His breath heaves, as he finds himself fighting off terrible emotion. He fears some sort of imminent breakdown. He wants out.

"Imagine what bright new world blinks awake, eyes lit by the fires of withered old ones burning," her voice says.

Whose voice? The suggestion emerges from himself.

Mark hesitates. What are the possibilities, once this door opens?

He'll be alone, and discover he always has been.

The others will have escaped while he lingered, trying to master his fears.

Maybe they'll be outside waiting, and with Mark they'll climb the stairs and go up to see the sky.

Polly and Greyson might want to leave, and Jenna will ask him to remain, just the two of them.

What else? There must be more possibilities.

But this is the only real ending, without the security of explanation and closure.

A new, harsh vibration pains his ears, sickening his gut. It's like touching the oscillating metal cylinder in Medical Center. A rising hum, too terrible to withstand.

He wants the universe to be stable and persistent, but everything is conflict, selfishness and agonizing disintegration.

This world is hungry to end.

Something feels different, but he can't see it yet. A future can't be held until it arrives. Each present moment is just a pinpoint, flashing too quickly in passing. All that exists and can be grasped is behind. The past moves slowly. Memory remains within reach, more vivid than perception.

Mark swings open the door and emerges, gun extended.

He faces a view of water, a flat blue mirror beyond scattered trees. It's not real, it's too perfect. It's all he can see, the same thing he sees every morning.

Uncertainty should be harder than knowing, but it's easier. Confusion is comfortable, proceeding with blank mind, each day pure vacancy.

Mark is ready to transform. Nothing exists beyond his eyes and his mind.

He hears others nearby, recognizes sounds of their movements, and familiar breathing. What remains? A view of water, and promise of escape. Someone to hope for, and a future that might eradicate the failures and despairs of yesterday.

"Remember, the new world is born in spring," someone says, the same woman's voice as before. How has he never known her?

Earlier, the other three transformed at least briefly, one at a time, into something they needed to be. Now it's Mark's turn.

Fear departs, resolve strengthens. He steps forward, gun raised toward the murmurs of friends. Yearning aches in him, a surge of hunger to touch someone else, the way trees extend limbs, straining for contact, a lonely grasping for another's hand. But there is no one else.

Four bullets. Enough to kill, enough to be born. Once he's done, he'll finally see what comes next.

END

ABOUT THE AUTHOR

Michael Griffin's latest collection *The Human Alchemy* (Word Horde) was a 2018 Shirley Jackson Award finalist. Other books include a novel, *Hieroglyphs of Blood and Bone* (Journalstone, 2017) and his debut collection *The Lure of Devouring Light* (Word Horde, 2016). His stories have appeared in Black Static and Apex magazines, and the anthologies *Looming Low, The Children of Old Leech* and the Shirley Jackson Award winner *The Grimscribe's Puppets*.

He's also an ambient musician and founder of Hypnos Recordings, a record label he operates with his wife in Portland, Oregon. His blog is at griffinwords.com

CPSIA information can be obtained
at www.ICGtesting.com
Printed in the USA
JSHW020328060223
37325JS00002B/165